OPULENCE
—KANSAS—

Julie Stielstra

D1400069

A MEADOWLARK BOOK

Meadowlark (an imprint of Chasing Tigers Press)
meadowlark-books.com
PO Box 333, Emporia, KS 66801

Copyright © 2020 Julie Stielstra

Cover photo by Jay Dee Miller, jaymillerphotography.com

All rights reserved.

This book and parts thereof may not be reproduced in any form, stored in a retrieval system, or transmitted in any forms by any means—electronic, mechanical, photocopy, recording, or otherwise—without prior written permission of the publisher, except as provided by United States of America copyright law.

This is a work of fiction. Names, characters, places, and incidents are the product of the author's imagination or are used fictitiously, and any resemblance to actual people living or dead, businesses, companies, events, or locales is entirely coincidental.

ISBN: 978-1-7342477-0-1

Library of Congress Control Number: 2019957376

To Leo and Theresia Feist,
who built a tall white house
in the middle of the Kansas prairie
over a hundred years ago.
Now it's a tall old yellow house,
where much of this story was written.

Thank you, Leo and Theresia.

OPULENCE

—KANSAS—

It was 9:32 AM by the wall clock when the principal's assistant, Ms. Fox, came to pull me out of World History. She wouldn't look at me. She murmured into Mr. Banks's ear, and his eyes swiveled straight to me, but she looked at the floor. No one said anything. I grabbed my stuff and followed her out. Usually they just sent a student runner for messages or appointments or whatever.

You've got to understand, I'm a good student . . . a "good girl," I guess. I get almost all A's, I don't smoke anything, and the only drinking I'd done is when Daddy poured me half a glass of Veuve Clicquot at New Year's. Something was really, really wrong.

"Did I do something?" I babbled. "I haven't done anything!"

"No no no no," said Ms. Fox. She stared straight ahead, clicking down the tile in her polished heels. She looked like Hillary Clinton, only with better hair. "There are some people who need to see you." And that was all she'd say. But she touched my shoulder.

Ms. Henne, the principal, was sitting at her desk. Ms. Snipe, the guidance counselor, was sitting in a chair. What was *she* there for? She was holding a box of Kleenex in her lap. They couldn't kick me out if I hadn't done anything, and besides (I remember everything seemed to take a long time, and I had time to think of all this stuff), if I was in trouble, they'd have my parents in there. Two strangers, a sandy-haired man in a baggy sports coat and a black woman in uniform, were sitting in the office. The woman had beautiful, gleaming cornrows.

The man stood up. "Katherine Myrdal?" he asked. I nodded. He held out a little case with an ID in it, but I just looked at his face. "I'm Detective Sergeant James Russell, Chicago Police, 4th district. This is Officer Tamberly Wallis."

What? What . . .

"What's wrong? What's happened?"

"I'm very sorry, Ms. Myrdal," Russell said. "There's no good way to tell you this. Your father is Lawrence Myrdal?" I swallowed and nodded again. "We got a call about a car in the lot at Rainbow Beach. We found him in the car. I'm afraid he's dead."

Rainbow Beach? Where the hell was Rainbow Beach? He kept the boat at Belmont Harbor . . . why would he be at Rainbow Beach?

"Katie . . ." Ms. Snipe stood up, clutching the Kleenex box.

"How . . ." I said.

"There was a note on the seat. It looks right now like he . . . like suicide."

"How," I said again. The two police looked at each other, at Ms. Henne, at me again.

"He shot himself," said Russell.

Where would he get a gun? Daddy didn't have a gun. Did he?

"Oh God," I said. "My mother . . ."

"We've informed her," said the policewoman. I couldn't think of her name. Did they tell me? "A friend is with

2

her, and she wanted us to come tell you and bring you home."

"Who is it, who's there?"

"Umm . . ." She opened her little notebook. This was like watching *Mystery*! on TV, for God's sake. "Jana Persimmon? She said she was her . . ."

"Oh, great," I groaned. "Her ditzy girlfriend. Her gluten-free all organic woo-woo girl."

"Katie . . ." said Ms. Snipe again.

The air around her was full of prickly little sparkles, little gray sparkles against dark gray walls in the dark gray air . . .

I hit my head on the edge of the desk on my way down.

They had me in a chair. Ms. Henne was kneeling in front of me, looking up into my face, holding out a cup of water.

"I am so, so sorry, my dear," she was saying. She stroked my hair back, I think to be sure I wasn't bleeding all over her office. But no, that's not fair. She was being gentle, and she was being as kind as you can be with a fainting sophomore in your office, who's just found out her Daddy has offed himself in his car on the beach someplace she's never even heard of.

I could hear the wailing before Jana Persimmon opened the door. And Mom was in her own bedroom at the other end of the condo. With the door closed.

"She's locked herself in," said Jana. "I gave her some chamomile tea and encouraged her breathing, but . . ."

It was like listening to an animal in a trap. Just this wordless, gasping howling. It was horrible. Could I just run away and come back when this was all over?

"We need to get her a doctor," said the policewoman. Officer Wallis, it was. I'd looked at her name badge.

"I have advanced-level credits from Bastyr University," said Jana. "If I can go home and get my bag . . ."

"Dr. Vargas lives on twelve," I said. "He's retired, but he'd come up." He was a nice man, had a little Havanese dog he was nuts about. I met them in the elevator sometimes. Officer Wallis left immediately.

"Mrs. Myrdal?" Russell was tapping, then rapping at the bedroom door. "Mrs. Myrdal? Are you all right? We're going to have a doctor come up. He can help you with . . ."

The door was ripped open.

I've never seen my mother look like that, before or since. Her whole face was twisted, her mouth this gaping hole, tears and snot on her face, yanking at her own hair.

"Why?" she shrieked. "Why would he do this? How could he do this?"

"We're going to try to find out what happened," said the cop. "You need to get some rest, and we'll come back tomorrow and talk to you then, okay?" Jana was peering over his shoulder.

"Katie!" wailed my mother. "Katie, what has he done to us?" She launched herself at me, and I hung onto her as she sobbed. There had to be something wrong with me, I know. I felt numb. If I'd been watching this in a movie, my heart would have been pounding, I might have even walked out. But this was for real; this was my mother, my dad, with death and suicide ringing around us, and I just stood there.

The thing was, my parents didn't really even get along.

Daddy worked long hours, traveled a lot, had a lot of

social stuff like business dinners and golf outings he went to. Mom did pretty much anything she wanted all day, every day: shopped, worked out, took yoga and meditation classes, was on all these committees and Friends' groups, like for the Art Institute and the symphony and the performing arts college. They just didn't do hardly any of it together. They'd go whole days and barely see or talk to each other. They didn't have big fights or anything—not in a long time anyway. We'd go out on the boat in the summers, usually with some clients of Daddy's, but that was about it.

Officer Wallis was back, with Dr. Vargas.

"Ms. Persimmon, if you would come along with me, please, and let this gentleman pass . . ." She was good. She got Jana Persimmon out of the hallway, and Dr. Vargas gently took my mother out of my arms and escorted her back into her room.

"I think," I said to Detective Russell, "I think I'd like to go lay down. Is that okay?"

"Which room is yours?" he asked.

I showed him.

It was supposed to be an "office or study." It was the smallest room in the condo, the only one that didn't have its own bathroom. It had a narrow strip of window, high up in the wall, so you couldn't really see out.

I felt safe in it.

When we first walked into the condo with the realtor, Daddy swept open the floor-to-ceiling living room curtains with a flourish. He was so thrilled. "Look!" he cried. "I can finally see some sky!" Nineteen stories below the pure glass wall, Lake Michigan swashed and tossed to the horizon and the vertigo nearly knocked me down. I stayed pressed against the far wall the whole time we were in there.

"It's okay, sweetheart," he told me. "We'll put in a wainscoting or something along the windows. It'll be fine."

I did get used to it. Sort of. But I kept to my safe little viewless room a lot.

"Do you want Dr. Vargas to come see you in a little bit?" Russell asked me.

"He's nice," I said. "Just to see him . . ."

"I'll tell him. You rest. We'll be back tomorrow, okay? And talk."

He left. I shut the door. I lay down on my bed. I stared at nothing. I didn't even cry. It was too weird. It got quiet for a while.

Tap tap.

"Katerina?"

"Okay," I said. The door opened and a little soft furry thing scrambled up on the bed: Dr. Vargas had brought Chica in to me. She danced and wiggled and licked my face. I hugged her, gulped, gasped, and began to cry. He petted us both sadly.

It got worse from there.

Chapter 2

It's bad enough when your father is dead. Even worse if he's killed himself. But imagine what it's like to see it on the newspaper front pages (the few that are left, anyway), on websites and newsfeeds, on the TV news, even mentioned on NPR and the Wall Street Journal. "Chicago financier found dead," "High-flying stockbroker probable suicide," "Advisor to the wealthy takes own life." They all ran one of two photos: one was the smiling, affable one with the red tie, the one you'd put on the annual report to make everyone feel everything was going just great; the other was the serious, leaning-in one with the blue tie, the one for the news profiles and interviews to show Lawrence Myrdal is a serious, in-charge guy. It was only a matter of hours before some of them started adding subtitles: "Financial dealings under investigation," "Company records sought," "What was he up to?"

Daddy! Daddy, what *were* you up to?

Detective Russell came back. He came in my room, left the door open, and sat at my desk with the chair turned around while I sat on the bed. Had my father been worried or anxious or depressed that I could see lately? I didn't know. I didn't think so. I didn't see him all that much. Had he said anything, just mentioned anything, about maybe business troubles? To me? Get serious. No.

Just pissed off about the general economy, like everybody else, I guess. Any unusual trips? Coming and going at funny hours? Phone calls? Not that I knew about. Nothing different, anyway.

"Look, Katie, I don't know that we can tell you why your dad did this. Our job is to figure out if anything illegal went on: like blackmail, or threats, or if someone else did this to him somehow, or if—I'm sorry to say this—he was doing something illegal himself and took this way out. If you think of anything that might help, call me." He stood up and gave me his card. Then he turned around and looked at the pictures on the wall over my desk.

I take pictures. I like taking pictures of secret, unnoticed things. Staircase shadows in an alley. The trickle of frozen sludge down the tile in the transit station. Graffiti on a rusty, peeling boxcar. I like to take pictures of stuff that when people look at them, they have to think to figure out what they're of. Hardly ever people. They work so hard to be noticed, or else they make this big deal out of not being noticed—like my mom. If anyone had a camera around, she'd fling up her arms and groan and squeal, "Don't you dare! I look so horrible!" so it just wasn't worth it for all the fuss. But somehow she always managed to smile and look cheery for the gala fundraiser dinner photos. But then she'd spent hours beforehand on her hair and makeup and dress for those.

Russell looked at the prints I had on the wall. He smiled a little. Then he looked at the one picture there was of a human.

"This your dad?" he asked.

"Yeah," I said. "Last summer. We were on the boat." With some clients. The guy and his wife were sitting around yakking with my mom. I was prowling around, taking pictures of water drops on the decking, the way the wood curved on the edge of the boat in places. I saw Daddy, standing at the rail by himself, around the corner from everybody else, and I just snapped the picture. He's leaning on the rail, staring at the water, with a beer bottle hanging in his fingers and his hair blown around with the sun on it. He was a handsome guy, Daddy was, even in his mid-fifties. It was a really nice picture. He heard the shutter snap and jumped.

"What the hell?" he said. Then he saw it was me. He kind of laughed then, and said, "Boy, I better be careful with you sneaking around like that. God knows what you'd catch me doing."

I did not tell Detective Russell any of that.

"Nice photos. The other thing is," he said, "just so you know . . . there are going to be accountants and lawyers, people like that, coming in and out for a while. They'll be going through business records, files, your dad's computers, to see if there's anything there we need to follow up. They'll mostly talk to your mom, I guess, but it doesn't seem like she was really involved in the business end, was she?"

I shook my head.

"Okay, then. You take care, and call me if there's anything that comes to you, anything that might help. Okay?"

"Okay," I said. He held out his hand and I shook it and he left.

Chapter 3

My mother slept. She took pills, she drank tea, and she slept. Or maybe not. But she stayed in her room and stumbled out once or twice a day for something in the kitchen. Even Jana Persimmon figured out that she wasn't going to fix this, which scared her away. Once, Mom wandered into Daddy's room and stood in his closet, just staring at his suits: his Armani suits, his Paul Smith suits, his custom-made shirts from Balani, and his beautiful polished English-made shoes, all perfectly neat in the closet.

I went in there and took one of the ties. I'd given it to him, from the Art Institute gift shop. He actually wore it quite a lot, even if it wasn't his usual $200 silk designer thing. It was a Klimt-y pattern of circles in ovals, in blue and aqua and turquoise, and it made his eyes glow those colors. I was glad he wasn't wearing it in the car that night. I tied it in a full Windsor knot (Daddy taught me how), and hung it on my bedpost.

I got my watch out too. The Rolex Lady-Datejust watch in rose gold with diamonds on the numerals. Daddy bought it for me for my last birthday.

"You're not a very blingy girl," he said. "So I didn't get the diamonds all the way around the edge. And I got a great deal on it." The edge is called the bezel—I looked it up online. And got nervous when I saw how much those

10

things cost. I was afraid to wear it, but I did for a while, and pulled my sweater sleeve down over it when I was on the street so no one would mug me for it. I admit, at school I pushed my sleeve up and let my arm lay kind of casually over my desk. I'm pretty sure Taylor Crandall sneaked a look at it, because later I heard her telling Monique Tattersall that she thought Patek Philippe watches were so much classier than Rolexes.

Whatever. Let's just say I don't exactly belong to the kind of clique where we gather around to squeal over each other's watch or earrings or manicure. In fact, I'm just not a group person. I guess I'm an introvert: I like to read (I was pretty into poetry for a while, but a good mystery hooks me too). I take pictures with a camera because I have like zero artistic talent except for *looking* at pictures. It just mystifies Mom, who's traveled in a pack since she was a kid: Girl Scouts and cheerleaders and student government and girls' nights out (which is how she met my dad), and now her classes and groups and committees. Besides her bedroom, she has a room all decorated with plants and rugs and candles and cushions, to be her "yoga and meditation room." She never uses it, never does any of it on her own, just goes to classes three times a week. Go figure.

Anyway, I got the watch out and put it on. It was beautiful. Heavy, smooth, with curves instead of squared edges. I had to press hard to get the clasp to click shut. It was the last present he bought me. I wished I'd worn it more.

The police came back, different ones. They went through Daddy's home office and took his laptop away with them. Then Detective Russell came back. Mom was getting a grip. She had showered and dressed, done up her hair and makeup. We sat in the living room. I curled up in the square red armchair like a box. Russell gave Mom a plastic envelope with a piece of paper inside. The one from the car. She glanced numbly at it and handed it over to me. It was so weird to see Daddy's big, squarish handwriting, the lines slanting down across the paper. Daddy was dead. Dead.

"I'm sorry. I can't keep it going any more. You'll be better off this way."

That's all it said. Not even his signature or initial or anything.

"Here's what we know," said Russell. "We got a call about a car in the lot at Rainbow Beach. Beach isn't open for the season yet, and frankly, a Porsche Cayenne is not what gets parked down there very often."

"Where is that?" I asked.

"South side," said Russell. "77th, 79th Street."

"What was he doing there?" murmured my mother.

"A kid out for an early run noticed the car, went to have a look at it. Saw your husband through the window and called. Paramedics knew . . . well, he was gone. The gun was in his hand. And the note. You all right? All right with this so far?"

Mom nodded. Whatever Dr. Vargas had been giving her must have been working.

"In the head?" she whispered.

Russell looked away, then nodded. "Yes, ma'am."

"Oh, God. The mess . . ." She'd gone white, and I just laid my forehead down on my knees. All I could think was how fussy he was about that car, having it washed and cleaned all the time . . . beige leather upholstery . . .

Russell cleared his throat.

"The guy who found him was kind of freaked out," he began. "Your husband had a hooded sweatshirt. He'd pulled it way up around his head, tied it up tight, and then, on top of that, he folded a big black towel around his head and shoulders. So the guy just saw this big bundle instead of his head . . ."

My mother made a little noise in her throat, and I just kept my head pressed hard on my knees with my eyes closed, but then I had to open them because all I could see was a big black bundle against the car window . . .

"It was like he was trying not to make a mess."

"Don't bring that car back," my mother babbled. "I don't want it, get rid of it, I don't want it back . . ."

"That's fine, Mrs. Myrdal. Don't worry about it, okay? It'll be taken care of however you want."

We all sat there for a minute. Russell waited. Then he said, "One more thing we need to talk about. The fraud team has been going through his office, his computers and so on. They found . . . found some questionable patterns. Things that didn't add up, didn't make sense. So we're getting some experts in—financial auditors, and now it looks like the federal securities commission may have to get involved. I guess I'm trying to let you know that it's looking like Larry Myrdal may have been . . . involved in . . . some seriously illegal business. Have you heard of a Ponzi scheme?"

My mother gasped.

"Like . . . like that Madoff man?" she asked, shakily. She was beginning to rumple her hair, pulling and twisting at it with her fingers.

"Afraid so. Not as big, not as good at it as Madoff, but the same idea. Taking people's money to invest for them,

13

then using that money to pay off other people's supposed investments. The investigation is going to take a while yet, but you have to know that all his assets are probably going to be frozen."

"They can't take this house away from us, can they? It's in our names, in some special way, he told me. And my car, my car, that's mine! And Katie's trust fund . . ." My mother was burbling, panicky. "He said if anything ever happened to him, it was the best way to be sure we were taken care of. They can't take it all away, can they?"

"The lawyers will have to figure that all out, Mrs. Myrdal. But in the meantime, you can't sell anything or move any accounts around or close them out, anything like that, till this is all worked out. Have you got a lawyer?"

"Yes, yes, of course. He's called already, he's coming to see me . . ." She trailed off and stared out the window. The sky was blue with thin puffy little clouds, like those old-fashioned bedspreads with little tufts in rows. "What about a funeral . . . or something . . .?"

Russell stood up. "Yes, ma'am. The manner of death seems to be established, so we can release him to you very soon. There will be other investigators in touch and may want to speak with you. And of course, call me if you have any other questions. I'm sorry for your loss, both of you. We will do our best to find out what happened."

As my mother closed the door behind him, she hissed, "Don't do us any favors, you sons of bitches."

I wished Dr. Vargas would give me some of that stuff.

Chapter 4

Mom was so *angry* after that. She did-n't want a funeral, didn't want a me-morial service, didn't even want to bury him.

"Just send the sonofabitch to the crematorium, straight from the morgue," she snarled.

I asked if I should go back to school. Or something.

"Sure. Fine. Just go right ahead, go on back to your life. So sorry you've been inconvenienced." She slammed the bedroom door.

I did not go back to school. I emailed Ms. Snipe. She emailed back she was sorry for my loss and not to worry. The year was nearly over anyway, and we could talk later about make-up work. At private schools, they cut you more slack, considering the tuition your parents pay them.

Jana Persimmon came slinking back around, and somehow, somebody organized a private funeral service, just to get it over with. There was me, Mom, Jana Persim-mon, and Daddy's secretary sobbing into endless Kleen-exes, a couple other people on Mom's committees, and this old couple I'd never seen before.

They sat on one of those hard brocade sofas at one side of the room. The man was very tall and lean, with a high bald head and fluffy gray eyebrows. The woman was short and chunky with long gray hair pulled back in a ponytail. They sat there together, quietly, looking uncomfortable. They made me think of that painting in the Art Institute, the farmer with the pitchfork and the sad-looking woman with him. But these people, they looked like the unhappiness wasn't normal to them, like they were usually pleasant people, but being here had made them different. I'd seen them speak to my mother, who was very formal and just shook their hands briefly.

"Who are those people over there?" I finally asked my mother.

She sighed and said, "Come on."

"Katie, this is Maggie and Len Myrdal. This is Katie. Katie, Len is your father's brother. Your uncle Len . . . and aunt Maggie." She seemed to run out of anything else to say, and turned away. I held out my hand, and the man stood up and took it in both his big bony ones. He looked at me for a long second and said, "My goodness. Oh, Katie Myrdal, you do favor your father." He dropped my hand and dropped himself heavily back down onto the sofa. He turned his face away and scratched at his left eye with his thumb. Maggie touched his arm. She stood up and hugged me.

"We're so sorry," she said into my ear.

I knew there was an older brother, like fifteen years older. But he lived back in Kansas, and there were Christmas cards and that was about it. I'd never met them. I didn't know anything more than that.

"You probably don't remember," said Len slowly, "when your mom and dad brought you out to the farm."

"They did? When?"

"You were just a little thing, maybe two years old? Just walking, anyway." He looked at Maggie, as though for confirmation. She smiled at him.

"That was before we met," she said.

"That's right," he said. "I forgot that. Seems like you've been around forever." She laughed softly.

"Anyway," he went on, "they were driving out to California to see your mom's people, and stopped to see me. Do you remember it at all?"

I shook my head. Not a bit.

"I remember your mom had you all dressed up in a little blue dress and sandal shoes. I took you out to show you the chickens and the calves, and she was so worried you'd get that dress dirty. And you did, of course." He chuckled a little. "You sat down in the grass and the chickens walked all around you, and you wanted to hug the calves and got slobber on you and you didn't mind a bit."

I'm sure I didn't care about getting the dress dirty. It was funny to think I had liked the chickens and calves. And it all sounded just like Mom. She probably wanted to show me off, and it didn't occur to her that a little-girl dress and sandals wouldn't exactly be the best thing to dress a toddler in to visit a farm.

"I wish I remembered it," I said. "It sounds like I liked it."

"You didn't stay long," said Len, eyes on the carpet. "We just kind of fell away after that, I guess. Your dad wanted out of there from the time he was a boy. He had big plans, big ideas, and he wasn't going to get anywhere in Opulence."

"Opulence? Is that the town you lived in?"

Len nodded. "Opulence, Kansas."

"Do you still live on that farm?"

"We do," he said. "Still live in the house my grandfather built."

"It's a funny old house," said Maggie. "It was his property I coveted when I married him."

Len smiled. "She's put in the biggest, most beautiful garden out there. I never had the time, but now it's fresh vegetables from April to November. Probably added years to my life." He took Maggie's hand and held it. We sat there for a little while.

"I'm glad you came all this way," I said. "I'm glad to meet you." Mom was beckoning me from across the room. They both stood up.

"If you ever want to come out to visit, you'd be more than welcome," Maggie said. "Take care of yourself and your mom."

Chapter 5

So that, in a way, is how I ended up getting off a plane at the Wichita airport, lugging shoulder bags with my laptop and my camera stuff. Len and Maggie were picking me up—they said they'd meet me at the baggage claim.

"Which one?" I'd asked.

Maggie had laughed. "Don't worry, we'll find you."

I live in Chicago, okay? Which means the airport I'm used to is O'Hare. Five terminals, like a hundred and fifty gates, and banks of screens with lists and lists of planes arriving and departing. Mobs of people, all in a hurry, lines into the restrooms, six dollar coffee and no place to sit. You have to look at more screens to figure out which baggage area your luggage will be at (hopefully), where you pay a buck to use a cart because it's like a mile to where your car is (if you can find it). So I get off in Wichita—with a dozen people—and walk out into this empty concourse. There were only two. We stroll along past a couple fast food places, down some stairs and there's the baggage claim. Just one. And there are Maggie and Len, and we wait about five minutes and there's my big suitcase.

Maggie already had a cart.

"I wasn't sure how much stuff you'd have," she said.

We trundled out the door, across the drive, and there's the parking lot (just one) and a big, red, dusty crew-cab pickup. Len set the suitcase in the back and held out a hand for my other bags.

"Um, this is my computer and camera stuff," I said. "Can I just keep it with me? You know, so it doesn't bounce around too much?"

"Sure," he said.

"You okay back there?" asked Maggie into the rear-view mirror. "Len needs to shove his seat back so far he'd squish you." She was driving.

"Oh, sure, I'm fine," I said. It was kind of cozy, curled up behind her as the truck rumbled along.

"Your flight was okay?"

"Yes, no problem."

Silence. We passed a Kmart and Walgreens and tire dealers and demolition companies and liquor stores. About like Roosevelt Road out in the suburbs. Flat. Bright. Sun ricocheting off windshields and chrome bumpers. I put on my sunglasses and was glad I had them.

"How's your mom doing?"

"Just . . . just getting along, I guess," I said. And thought, what have I done? Why am I driving along in a pickup truck with two total strangers, to go stay in their farmhouse in God-knows-where-Kansas? Didn't that whole *In Cold Blood* thing happen in Kansas? Why did this seem like a good idea?

But I knew why.

Anything to get out of that house, away from my furious, miserable, confused mother. Who was only too glad to be rid of me so she could do or be or say whatever she had to in the wreckage.

"We're glad to have you, hon," said Maggie. "I hope it's a good thing for both of you. Let's take 96," she said to Len. "Show her something besides the interstate."

"How far is it to your house?" I asked.

"Couple hours," said Len. "Hundred miles or so."

"Oh my God," I said. "A hundred miles to pick me up at the airport?"

"Everything's farther apart out here!" said Maggie. Her eyes in the mirror were smiling. "From what I heard, it can take that long to get across town in Chicago."

Well, that's true.

"It's okay," she said. "Len had a doctor's appointment in Wichita this morning, so we came down last night, saw some old friends, got the doc seen, then came and got you. All worked out nicely. Scissor-tailed flycatcher!"

Len smiled. "You and your birds."

Maggie pulled the truck over on the shoulder. I craned around, looking behind for the traffic to back up . . . there wasn't any.

"There!" she said, pointing. A huge empty green field stretched away, with barbed wire tacked to fenceposts made of tree branches and a gateway with a bar across tall posts, like out on the range. On the high cross rail there was a bird sitting, about robin-size, maybe, with a long, long tail.

"My favorite bird," she said. "They have the most beautiful peach-colored breast, and when they fly, that tail opens and closes and swirls. Must be a good sign, to see one when you've just come." She pulled the truck back onto the blacktop, and we rumbled off again.

A few more miles of quiet.

"Did you say you had a computer with you?" Maggie said.

21

"My laptop and my iPad," I said. Oh my God. What if they didn't have internet access? I'd have no email, no access to my photo stream . . . Maggie's eyes slid sideways to Len and crinkled.

"See," she said to him. "I told you that fiber optic connection was a good idea."

"She's the computer expert," said Len.

I smiled. Whew.

"Cellphone service can be a problem, though, just to warn you," said Maggie. "But if you stand right next to the window in your room upstairs, sometimes you can get a signal."

"Or out by the mailbox," offered Len.

I must have looked a little shocked because Maggie said, "Don't worry, there's a landline. In case somebody falls off the windmill or something."

We hadn't had a landline in, like, years. It might actually be better. I could just email Mom. And not have to actually talk to her . . . I got out my cellphone, and there was a signal. I texted Mom.

All OK. On way to farm

Minutes pass.

Ping.

OK Then, ping: *Be good guest*

Okay, well, so much for that.

I sat back in the seat. Len and Maggie seemed to be people not bothered by silence. We just rolled quietly along, past emerald green expanses cut through with little creeks and streams, lined with shaggy trees. I'd thought Kansas would be flat and gray—too much *Wizard of Oz*, I guess. But it wasn't, not here anyway. The land had a shape, sort of bones and muscles under the grass, sloping here and valleys there. Red and gold clouds were bunching and rising up in the distance.

"Supposed to storm tonight," said Len.

"May in Kansas," said Maggie.

I mean, I didn't expect exciting conversation. But it was, I don't know, restful in the back seat of the red truck, big thick tires gripping the road, facing the towering colored clouds.

You could see a long way out here. From the ground.

Chapter 6

The house was tall and yellow and old. The sun lit up one side of it to a butter color, the rest of it shady inside a square of raggedy, splintery trees. A couple scuffed-up metal chairs, painted red like the trim on the house, sat in the yard outside the door with a rusty little table and a camping lantern hung on a pole between them.

"Have to find you a chair," said Len.

"Thrasher!" cried Maggie as a big brown bird swept across the driveway. "He always comes to say hi."

As we got out of the truck, a red chicken came bustling out from behind the garage.

"A chicken!" I cried. "Is it yours?"

"She is," said Maggie. "This is Celeste. There's more of them around. That can be your job while you're here. Feed 'em, get the eggs, let 'em out, shut 'em up at night. Chickens are nice. They'll like you."

Me? The chickens would like me?

Maggie scooped up the little red chicken at her feet and handed her to me. She showed me how to hold her, and this funny warm body with scratchy feet just sat there in the crook of my elbow and made soft chortling noises.

"Told you," she said. "She's a little needy since the coyote got her sister."

24

How do you pet a chicken? Well, she didn't seem to mind however I did it.

Len took my suitcase inside. There were irises by the door.

My room was upstairs. It had creased flowery wallpaper with blue and silver stripes and three tall windows with no curtains. Two of them looked right into the trees, and one looked out over the fields to the west. We'd passed one house down the road a ways; Maggie said that was the Kirchners, the nearest neighbors. Sitting on the squeaky high bed—the kind with a white tubular metal frame like hospital beds in old movies—I felt like I was in a treehouse. There was a big old oak desk with dry, groany drawers, and my laptop looked quite perky and modern sitting on it. I took a picture of the room on my cellphone, then stood right by the window and sent it to Mom, with one flickering bar of service. It went, though. I don't know if she answered or if the message just didn't come. I didn't really care. Not really.

After dinner, Maggie asked me if I drank coffee. She was filling up a steel pot with water, and fitting it up with a tube and a little metal basket.

"Oh, yeah," I said. "I really need my coffee in the morning. What kind of coffee maker *is* that, anyway?"

Maggie looked at the pot, then at me.

"Umm, it's a coffeepot," she said. "You know, a percolator?"

"A what?" Mom had three different kinds of coffee makers: a Bunn drip, a French press, and a big shining espresso thing with valves and spigots and stuff that she wouldn't let me use.

Maggie laughed, and I felt stupid.

"You put the coffee in here, like this, then just turn the stove on. The water boils, up through here, then drips back down . . . you've never seen one?"

"No, I guess not."

Maggie put a big red plastic jug of coffee back in the cupboard. Already ground, grocery store stuff. Well, there probably wasn't a Starbucks for miles. It'd be coffee . . . caffeine. I could be polite about it. Maybe I could buy them a grinder and order some beans online and show them the good stuff.

Then we put the chickens to bed. There were ten of them, all girls.

"Last roo we had went for Len, and we ate him for Sunday dinner," Maggie explained. "Too much trouble."

"Don't you need a rooster . . .?" I felt stupid again.

"Only if you want chicks. The girls do eggs just fine all by themselves."

Well, I remembered the "Growing into a Woman" class in fourth grade, and they showed about eggs passing through and out, so I guess that made sense.

There were red hens and speckled hens and some big tan ones. Buff Orpingtons, they were called.

"Sounds like a preppy kid from Lake Forest," I said.

Maggie laughed. "I should call them Missy and Heather."

"And Jennifer," I added. "Or Taylor or Madison."

"Too late," said Maggie. "That's Myrtle, that one's Verna, and this one is Dinah. Come on, ladies, chick-chick-chick! Go on, call 'em."

"Chicky chick chick!" And they all came hustling and clucking. I poured the scratch into the feeder in the hen house, and they scrambled inside.

Maggie locked up the door. "Eggs for breakfast. Eggs for breakfast, actually, pretty much every day now. Glad you're here to help us eat them. And quiche. And frittatas. And cakes . . ."

"Will you show me?" I asked.

"Sure! Do you cook much at home?"

"Not really. Mom and Daddy, their schedules are all over the place . . . were . . . we just . . ."

Suddenly I was in tears. I wanted pad thai chicken . . . no, wait, not chicken . . . shrimp instead. And baklava. And a giant latte. And my dad. And, so help me, my mom. And my little cave of a room, with blinds I could close with a long stick.

Maggie put her arms around me, with her chin on my head.

"Look," she whispered. "Look at the sun."

We turned around. The whole sky was lit up in scarlet and turquoise and purple, great messy streaks and swatches of it. I wiped my eyes on my sleeve. And thought, tomorrow I will set up my camera and take pictures. Maybe . . . every single night, at sunset, I'll take a picture. In a series, at exactly the same moment, from the same exact spot. The scalding sun drifted down, and in moments, it was gone. Then Len was standing with us, and we watched the colors flare even brighter, then fade.

"Still saying it's gonna storm tonight," he said.

"I hope it does," I said.

It did, too. I woke up when the wind suddenly tore through the trees. I couldn't understand what those tall rectangles were, pale against the dark, until I figured out they were the windows and I wasn't in Chicago any more.

27

WONK – WONK – WONK! I nearly jumped out of my skin when this shrill honking wailed outside my room. Then a disembodied male voice started chanting robotically from somewhere . . . My door opened and I cried out.

"Oh, hon, I'm sorry!" said Maggie, filling the doorway in a baggy nightgown. "It's the weather radio, is all. Here, come on."

I felt like an idiot for about the tenth time in the last twenty-four hours. From a little box on the table in their bedroom, the voice droned on about a severe thunderstorm reported east of Kingman heading northeast at forty-five miles per hour with hail up to one half inch and wind gusts up to fifty miles per hour damage to roofs and siding to be expected . . . Maggie punched the off button.

Len was sitting up in bed, his ruff of hair every which way, blinking.

"Should have warned you," said Maggie. "Scares the crap out of me too, every time. But better to know what's coming out here. This one's no problem—it'll pass by us. But we're going to get the edge of it . . . here it comes."

The sky lit up, the thunder erupted, and out of nowhere the rain slashed in. Maggie closed the windows. My heart was still thumping. Len nestled back down with his back to us, but Maggie and I stood at the window and watched the illuminated trees thrashing.

"You get some big winds in Chicago, too, don't you?" she asked.

"At home, on the 19th floor, when it blows hard, you can see the water sloshing in the toilet," I said. "The whole building sways a little . . ."

"Good God!" cried Maggie. "That would scare me!"

"Me too," I confessed. "This feels more . . . steady."

"I hope so," she said. "At least it's not so far to fall. I figure, if this house has stood here for a hundred years, it'll probably hang on a bit longer for us. I'll turn the volume down on that thing so you can go back to bed."

So I did.

In the morning, I woke up with the sun glowing outside. Eight fifteen—I *never* woke up that early. There was an insulated mug on the bedside table with an insurance agent's name on it. The coffee tasted fantastic—hot and rich and not charred. There must be something to that percolator thing.

I padded down the stairs barefoot.

"Katie!" Maggie called softly, but urgently. "Quick, come see!"

She pointed out the big south bay window in the living room. In the front yard there were a dozen birds—tall, lean, brown birds with tiny heads stalking and strolling around the bushes.

"Turkeys," she murmured.

"Wow," I said. "You have turkeys *and* chickens?"

She laughed. "They're not ours. These are wild ones."

I stared. One of the turkeys suddenly puffed himself up all big and tipped up his tail into a fan—exactly like the silly Thanksgiving candles we had when I was little. He marched around like Mr. Big Shot, but the other turkeys—the girls—just wandered around picking up stuff in the grass. One of them was stretching up on tiptoe, trying to reach some little blossom or something high up in one bush, making little hops to try to get to it. We laughed.

Wild turkeys and blazing sunsets and midnight robot voices and massive thunderstorms and delicious coffee from a plain old pot. I was definitely not in Chicago any more.

"Go throw on some jeans," said Maggie, "and let's see what the chickens have for our breakfast."

And I learned how to make an omelet.

Chapter 7

"So," said Maggie, as she put away the skillet. "How do you feel about going to church?"

My immediate, thoughtful, gracious response was to stare at the dish towel and go, "Um."

"It's okay," she said. "You don't have to. I don't always go either, but Len likes to. 'Some keep the Sabbath going to church, I keep it staying at home . . .'"

I started. I remembered that poem! From my Emily Dickinson period . . .

"'With a bobolink for a chorister and the orchard for a dome,'" I said.

Maggie picked it up: "'God Himself preaches the sermon, and the sermon is never long . . .'"

"'So instead of getting to heaven at last, I'm going all along!'" we finished together and laughed. Wow. Just this nice feeling of pure pleasure, just being with someone, doing the dishes and saying an old poem.

"After the service, we're having a picnic—for Memorial Day."

I'd forgotten it was Memorial Day weekend. And instantly felt terrible—I was out here, laughing in the kitchen with Maggie, while my mom was going to be languishing alone over my dad's ashes . . . but she probably wasn't.

"Oh, hell, I am so sorry," Maggie said. "I didn't think . . . Oh hell . . ." She stood nervously wringing at the dishrag.

I liked how she swore.

"It's okay," I said. "I forgot too. Now I feel bad. I shouldn't have forgotten, it's all just so weird . . . Part of me is glad when I forget, and then I feel guilty, but I can't help it . . ." I trailed off.

Maggie wiped back a straggle of her hair. "Anyway," she said, "the church is hosting a picnic with the social service in town—for kids and families with problems, you know? Battered women or kids with parents who died or who are gone in the military—just any family with kids who need some help. I don't know, would you want to come? Help out, meet some of the neighbors? Maybe—if you didn't mind, maybe you could bring your camera and take some pictures? Just for the folks who'll be there, they might like some snaps . . ."

Church picnics are not exactly my thing, obviously. Mom was raised Catholic, I think, but Daddy wasn't anything, or that's what he always said. I don't think I ever went to church. But when we studied the Middle Ages in school, I always kind of liked the stuff about the monasteries. Quiet, orderly, simple: you prayed and ate and worked all at certain times, and it was silent. And modest.

"Really, it's fine if you don't want to. But you'd be absolutely welcome to come."

"Sure," I said. "I'll come. I don't have any church clothes, though."

She laughed. "The pastor'll be in jeans under his robe. God sure doesn't care."

Why not? And if I took a few pictures of people and their kids, why not?

I liked the singing. The hymn books had all the words for you and everyone else knew the melody, and somehow the tunes were so . . . I don't want to say predictable, exactly, but there was something simple and direct about them, that even I could kind of tell where the lines would go, and after a verse or two I could sing along. Singing with people—another nice thing I never expected.

Afterward, I was introduced to Pastor Dave, a ruddy-faced graying man who shook my hand and said simply, "Bless you and welcome!" He was in fact wearing jeans—and work boots—under his robe. He took off his robe to come into the gathering hall to help set up tables and the men all heaved the tables around with much screeching and scraping of metal and linoleum. More people started coming in with a burst of kids' and women's voices, and there were smells of casseroles and salad dressing and onions. Someone started frying up hamburgers. We stayed inside because the clouds were piling up again, shot through with blazes of sunshine that came and went. I tagged after Maggie, who introduced to me the Kirchners and a bunch of other people, and many of them had the same last names, and I lost track of who was who. They were all very nice and smiled at me and said they were glad to meet me. They did not ask what grade I was in or how long was I staying, though everyone did manage to make some kind of wry comment about how different this must be from Chicago. And every time I said—honestly—that yes, it was different and in a good way. That made them happy, and overall it was pretty easy.

It was like people out here knew how to live with space between them. In the city, there are so many people all in the same place that you storm along and grab your own space before anyone else can take it and act like there's no one else there. And then, when you're with people you *do* know, it's all hugs and air kisses and over-sharing about your diet and other people's marriages and the state of your bowels, for all I know. Out here, there was plenty of space for everybody, so you were actually glad to see each other as it happened, and chat and have a friendly word, and then leave spaces for breathing. I was a total stranger, but that was *okay*.

I got out my camera, and Maggie started lining people up, and I took their pictures, and they all just stood there grinning, and it was no big deal. She knew who every-body was, so we'd sort through the shots later on. I took some candid party shots, just for the heck of it, and then went to find the bathroom. It was down a windowed hall-way, and when I came around the corner, I saw a guy sit-ting on a bench. He didn't notice me. He looked about my age, maybe a little older, so maybe not so into the mom-and-kids theme that afternoon. He sat hunched for-ward, his elbows on his knees, intent on his cellphone. The sun emerged from the clouds and suddenly rim-lit him: outlined his shape, the curve of his back, the angles of his elbows and shins, light on his forearms and the toes of his boots. I snapped off three shots and the sun disap-peared. He still hadn't seen me. The bathroom was right opposite where he was sitting. When I got there, he glanced up and I said, "Hi." And went into the bathroom. I felt embarrassed that he could hear me flush the toilet. He said hi to me when I came out again. What the hell.

"Hi," I said again. "I'm Katie, Katie Myrdal."

"Oh, right. Len and Maggie's, what, niece, right?" I guess word travels fast.

"Yeah. Nice to meet you."

Silence.

"Did you get, like, something to eat or anything?" I asked him.

"Naw, no, thanks. I just brought my little brother to this thing. My mom had to work, so I said I'd bring him."

"Oh. Which . . . which one is your brother?"

"Fat little dude in camo pants." I knew who he meant. "He's Doug. I'm Travis. Travis Gibb."

Then he turned his head. His hair was shaggy, just un-cut long, not on-purpose long, but not all over. The right side of his head was almost bald, just a feathery fuzz, with a few strands off the top falling down. The skin was stiff, shiny, pink, creased, and he didn't really have a right ear, just a gnarly little rim around the ear hole. I felt a little sick, but was damned if I'd let on. The pink shiny skin sheath went down his neck inside his collar. And his right hand . . . curled, contracted, two fingers missing. He placed his hand by his thigh where I couldn't see it.

"Burns," he said. "You haven't heard the Gibb house fire story yet?"

I shook my head.

"Your dad, I heard he died," he said.

I nodded.

"I'm sorry," he said. "So did mine."

"In the fire?"

This time he nodded. "Back in January."

"But you and your other family are okay?"

"Mom was working. Thank God. I got Dougie out, and he was fine. But my dad . . . he was done. Nothing to do for him."

35

"My dad shot himself," I said abruptly. What, was this some kind of competition? Whose dad had the most gruesome death?

"I heard that," he answered. I stood there, twisting my camera strap, while Travis Gibb sat there and looked up at me. "It'll get easier," he said. "Takes a while, though. Maybe not so bad for me. My dad was a son of a bitch."

"Mine wasn't!" I said. "Not to me."

He stood up.

"I better go find Dougie," he said. "See you around, I guess. Maggie and Len are good people. They'll take good care of you."

And he walked away.

Chapter 8

From the back seat, I said, "I met a guy, Travis Gibb. D'you know him?"

"Oh, lord, yes," said Maggie. "The fire. What a terrible thing that was. They were so lucky those boys got out."

"No thanks to their old man," said Len. There was a hard edge in his voice I hadn't heard before. He stared out the window and muttered something like "riddance."

"Len! He paid an awful price."

Len turned to look at her and said, "Oh, come on, Maggie. Rollie Gibb was cooking meth and everybody knew it. He had it coming. I'm just thankful he was in the bathroom with the door shut so he was the only one incinerated. If he'd been in the kitchen in that little house, they'd've all burned."

He looked out the window again. I sat in the back. Maggie gripped the steering wheel. With her eyes in the mirror on me, she said, "Travis is a good kid. I never heard any bad about him."

"A miracle," said Len. "Why Joanie put up with Rollie all this time . . . she works two, three jobs to get by, waitressing and tending bar and I don't know what all, with those boys to raise. My God, the lives that man has ruined . . . Travis was a decent point guard and a helluva pitcher—K State was looking him up and down for scholarships. And now, with that hand burned to a crisp, pffft.

He'll be working the rental counter at the farm supply store the rest of his life."

"He's a smart boy," said Maggie. "He could do something else. He doesn't have to rely on sports for everything."

"Without the scholarship? Ha."

Then he reached over and touched Maggie's leg.

"I don't mean to be fighting with you," he said. "But that Rollie, he was always bad news and that makes me furious."

"Maybe my dad wasn't so squeaky clean either," I said. "Just a different class of crook."

"Now, we don't know that . . ." "They don't have all the facts yet . . ." They both spoke at once.

"If he wasn't into anything bad," I snapped, "then he didn't need to shoot himself in the head, did he. And abandon us. Abandon me."

Len was looking over his shoulder at me. "Hon, this is not your fault. Not at all."

"Not Travis's fault either," I muttered. "It's like you're writing him off because of his dad." And I know I thought—or was afraid—they might be writing me off the same way.

"'Course not," he said. "I didn't mean it that way. He's just paying for the sins of his father. Shouldn't be that way, but it is sometimes." He turned back to the window. "And too many other people been paying for the sins of Rollie Gibb, all his goddamn life."

Nobody said anything else the rest of the way home.

I went upstairs and downloaded the pictures from my camera. They were nice enough—busy, cluttered, but people were smiling, and they'd like them. There was a pretty nice one of Maggie talking to Pastor Dave—he was gesturing and she was laughing and it kind of caught them and the feel of the afternoon. And then there was one of Travis—one of the three. It was one of those rare times when the picture on the screen almost matched up with what was in my head when I shot it. The light, the shadows, the geometry of his body, even a whispery glow from his cellphone—it all came together. I cropped it just a little bit.

Tap tap at the door.

"Katie?"

I clicked over to the shot of Maggie and Dave and said, "Come on in."

Maggie stuck her head in. "You okay with just soup and a sandwich or something for supper? We kind of pigged out at the church."

"Sure, fine. Look, look here—you'll like this one."

She did. We clicked through some of the others.

"We can put them on the church Facebook page!" I said. "If people say it's okay, I mean."

"Umm, I doubt Pastor Dave knows what that is," said Maggie.

"Aw, too bad. I bet people would like it."

"You can ask him . . . you could set it up, right?"

"Sure. No big deal, just, you know, basic information and announcements and pictures and stuff like that. I'd be glad to."

She stroked my hair.

Len called up the stairs that the soup was going to boil over, and we went down.

After dinner, he came out to where I was setting up my tripod for my sunset picture. The clouds were still piling up, but it hadn't rained, so we were going to get another one of those big, splashy, gory sunsets. He tacked a couple little pegs in the ground where my tripod legs were.

"That way you'll get it set exactly the same way every time," he said.

We were okay again.

Chapter 9

That week I helped Len tear down a fence. It was an old stretch of fence between the barn and a shed, a pretty sad shambles of barbed wire and chicken wire and broken boards and even some baling twine. I saw exactly what people meant when they said something was "held together with bubble gum and baling twine." Even though Len was out of the cattle business himself, the Kirchners would bring over half a dozen cows and calves in the spring to run on a few acres of his grass, and then Len got some beef for the trouble.

"And I don't have to mow this part," he added.

But last fall the cows busted through that place in the fence, and it was just as well, he said, it was way past time to fix it right anyway.

"Wait!" I said. "Let me take some 'before' pictures!" I got my camera and took some shots of Len leaning his elbow on a crooked post, and then some close-ups of the wiry tangle tacked to a split, weathered old post. "Okay, now we can tear it down, and I'll take more when it's all finished."

"You need some gloves, young lady," he said. "Go ask Maggie to find you some."

She gave me a pair of her gardening gloves, which were too big, but the leather palms kept the rusty barbs from puncturing me. Len gave me a fencing tool, with points and jaws and cutting places, and we just started ripping out nails and staples and rusty wire. I got to try to coil up the barbed wire, and it wanted to twist and whip back at me, but I wrestled it around, unstuck it from my jeans, and got it wound up nice and neat like a big spiky wreath. We threw all the junk in the back of the truck, and then piled it into another shed where there was another heap of metal posts and screen and fencing and rusted stuff. Len said we'd take it all to the scrap yard sometime. Then he decided we were going to need to replace five or six posts, so he showed me how to put chains around them, and he pulled them out of the ground with his truck. "Which is one reason why we don't set 'em in cement," he explained. We put the old posts over by the woodpile, and they'd get cut up and burned in the woodstove in the winter.

"You ever use a chainsaw, Katie?" he asked me. The way I must have looked at him made him laugh. "It's okay, hon, just teasing you."

Then we measured out where he wanted to put the new post holes and stuck stakes in there to mark them.

"Enough for today," he said. "Start digging new holes tomorrow. This girl," he said to Maggie, "we need to keep her."

"Fine by me," said Maggie.

I can't tell you how good that made me feel. And how sore I was the next morning. Funny how I didn't think it was that hard when I was doing the work. Len was helping and I was concentrating on what we were doing. But in the morning, my shoulders and across my chest and even my legs were telling me all about it! I didn't say a thing to Maggie or Len, though. I went and let the chickens out and found four new eggs. As I was coming back into the yard, Maggie came striding in through the gate, looking mad. Len was over by the fence, starting to hack at the ground.

In the kitchen, she clenched her fists and her teeth, rolled her head back and made that pissed-off growl you do deep in your throat when you are just so frustrated . . . "ERRRGGGHH!" she growled. "Stubborn, stupid!"

I started very quietly brushing dirt off the eggs.

"I'm sorry," she sighed. "But he's out there, thinking he's going to dig those postholes by himself with that old clamshell digger. His back's bad enough—he is NOT going to dig those holes that way! But will he listen? No! Dammit. Well, I'll just have to override him." She picked up the phone and punched in a number she obviously knew by heart.

"Tool rental, please," she said. "Yeah, hi, this is Maggie Myrdal . . . Travis, yeah, hi, how are you? Good . . . listen, have you got an auger of some kind on hand? Yeah, for post holes . . . right, yes, an earth drill. Oh, a one-man, I guess, that's all I got here." She rolled her eyes at me and grinned. "Tomorrow, huh. Okay, well, that'll be okay. I'll try to keep him out of trouble till then. Would you, really? Oh, that'd be great—thanks a lot. No, nothing else we need . . . no, wait, can you bring some work gloves, you know, the yellow cowhide kind? Mine are too big . . . yeah, medium should work. Great. Sure, I'll tell her. Take care, see you tomorrow. Thanks!"

She hung up and retied her pony tail. "If we can keep Len from killing himself today, Travis'll bring a gas-power drill over tomorrow. He says hi, by the way." She smiled at me, and then sighed. "He really is a nice kid. Poor Travis. Hope life gets better for him soon."

"Me too," I said.

Maggie made Len put up a new clothesline for her in the back yard after lunch. He'd been pretty silent at the table, and when I peeked out at the fence, I could see that he wasn't exactly punching his way to China with that post hole digger. While we were stringing the new cord between the poles, an old two-tone pickup truck came clanking into the drive. Travis Gibb, in a baseball cap, got out and yanked open the tailgate. Len and I trailed out towards him, and Maggie met him in the drive.

"Where d'you want this thing?" Travis asked Len. Len looked at Maggie and sighed.

"I thought you weren't going to have one till tomorrow," Maggie said.

"Guy brought it back early," said Travis, "so I figured I'd run it over now. If we get those holes dug quick, I can slip it back tonight, and . . ."

"We'll pay for it," said Maggie firmly. "But it'll be great to get it done so fast."

"No problem," said Travis. "I wrote it all up anyway. These okay?" He tossed two pairs of gloves at me. One pair was thick, yellow, stiff hide; the other pair had a thinner stretchy fabric—in periwinkle blue—on the backs, and gray rough-textured leather on the palms.

"For me?"

"You'll be glad you have them," said Maggie. I pulled on the heavy ones and flexed my fingers. "They'll break in," she said.

"Thought you could use the other ones for lighter stuff," said Travis.

I looked from one to the other. "Thanks."

Travis pulled his truck over by the fence line, and he and Len wrestled this giant drill out of it. Maggie gave me a look and I followed her.

"Let him save face," she said. "They'll be done in no time now."

They dug all five holes in an hour or so. Travis drove off with the drill without saying goodbye. I wondered how he knew the gloves were for me.

Chapter 10

When I get back to Chicago, I thought, maybe I'd leave my blinds open at night. Having the morning light come in, like it did here, maybe I'd keep getting up early. It made the day seem longer, more time to do stuff.

I shuffled down the stairs with my insurance agent mug, which was miraculously at my bedside every morning. There were voices in the kitchen: Travis Gibb was sitting at the kitchen table, baseball cap hung on the chair back, while Len (*Len?*) was swirling pancake batter at the stove. And there I am, standing there in my baggy plaid jams and an old T-shirt, no bra . . . oh geez.

"You want syrup or preserves on your pancakes?" asked Maggie.

"Umm, preserves," I said.

"Strawberry or apricot?"

"Apricot! Oh, I haven't had that since we were in Paris and they gave it to us every morning with bread for our breakfast."

Travis glanced at Maggie. She looked at me. "Good choice," said Maggie. "From our own trees out back. Apricots a la Kansas."

Maybe I shouldn't have said that. About Paris. Well, it was true!

"Travis said he'd give us a hand with the fence today," said Len, sliding more cakes onto a platter.

"Is school out for you here?" I asked.

He nodded. "We get done earlier here," he said. And shoveled in some pancake.

I bolted upstairs to get dressed, even if my pancakes got cold.

First, I tamped. Len set the posts and leveled them so they were perfectly vertical; Travis shoveled dirt down the hole. I took a thing that looked like a narrow hoe and packed the dirt down. Whack, whack, thump, thump, pack, pack, till it was tight and hard and smooth. Then Travis shoveled in a little more dirt and I tamped some more. When the hole was filled in, those posts didn't budge. Amazing what packed dirt can do.

Then Len showed me how to use the Skilsaw. Set those boards on the sawhorses, measure out the length they told me, mark it with a pencil along an L-shaped square so it was perfectly straight, fire up the saw and cut.

"Measure twice, cut once," said Len. So I did. Exactly. I think Travis was laughing at me. Or tolerating me. Or something. But I was damned if I'd screw up and let him think I was useless. He didn't say a word, but I was getting this vibe, that here I was, this rich city girl, trying to pretend she was . . . well, I don't know what exactly, but pretending. So I measured and cut those two by eights (that helped, I knew what to call the boards now!) *exactly* as they said, and they nailed them up.

After the fourth one, I got a little flit of sawdust or something in my eye and pulled off my glove to rub it. I saw my bare arm, a little tan already, and realized my watch was gone. I looked at the other wrist, but of course it wasn't there. Maybe I hadn't put it on . . . maybe it was sitting on the desk in my bedroom . . .

"Be right back," I said. And walked—fast—into the house and straight upstairs, and, of course, it wasn't there.

I'd lost it. Maybe it popped off when I was tamping, and it was gone down a post hole. I shouldn't have been wearing it. How stupid could I be? Wearing a Rolex to build a fence? No wonder Travis despised me. Maggie and Len would despise me. But I had to look for it, I had to.

I dragged myself back out there. Len and Travis were swigging from cans.

"Umm," I said. They looked at me. "I lost my watch . . . out here, somewhere . . ."

"What's it look like?" Travis was scanning the ground.

"Gold, with . . . diamonds on it . . ."

"Aw, Katie," said Len. "I coulda told you not to wear that, not to work in!"

"I know," I said miserably. He tried not to show it, but the corners of Travis's mouth flexed down, and his eyes— oh, just such a little bit—rolled.

"I know," I said again. "But . . . but my dad gave it to me. It was the last present he bought me . . ."

God forgive me. It was cheap. It was true but not honest. But it worked.

Len said, "Well, hell. If it's down a post hole, Katie, we're not gonna pull 'em up again."

"I know." Again. I knew a lot for someone so stupid.

Len and I started circling the posts, kicking the loose dirt, sweeping the grass aside with our feet.

And there was Travis, standing in front of me, the gold bracelet glinting as it hung from his gloved finger.

"Oh! You *found* it! Oh my God. Where was it?" I cried. I took it from him and stuffed it deep into my jeans pocket. I never wanted to wear it again, I was so embarrassed.

"By the sawhorses," he said. "Maybe it pulled loose when you took off your glove."

"Thank you," I said, a little shaky. "Thank you so much." And I hugged him. And he hugged me back.

He did. And patted my back, and let me go, and smiled.

"Always glad to help," he said. "Now, you want to cut another board or two or is it time for lunch yet?"

Len looked at his watch, a battered black plastic ten-dollar digital deal, and said, "Lunch. And put that damn thing somewhere safe."

I took the watch upstairs and zipped it up in one of the inside pockets of my laptop bag. At least it'd be safe there till I got back to Chicago.

"The clasp is wonky," I told them when I came back down. "It just doesn't catch."

"Maybe Marla can fix it?" said Travis.

"That's the jewelry store in town," said Maggie. "Couldn't hurt to have her look at it, next time we're there."

"Okay," I said. "Whenever." And we ate our egg salad sandwiches.

Chapter 11

"Len," said Maggie, "you should show Katie your grandfather's old watch sometime."

We were sitting out in the old chairs in the dark, with moths flicking around the hissing camp lantern. Maggie had pointed out the shapes of the bats glimmering around the big farm light on the barn, where the bigger prey was.

"I don't think I even know where it is," said Len.

"Top right drawer of the dresser in our room upstairs," said Maggie promptly. "I'm about ready to go in anyway."

Len tweaked off the lamplight and we straggled inside.

At the dining room table, he handed me a small square white box.

"It was actually my great-great grandfather's watch," he said. "I think he got it a little while after the war, and gave it to his son when my granddad was born."

That was enough to make my head spin . . . how long ago was that?

"After World War Two?" I guessed.

Len laughed. "The Civil War, hon!"

Wow. The watch—an old-fashioned pocket watch— was wrapped loosely in a plastic bag. It was thick and heavy and glossy, and the roundness fit snugly into my palm. There was a sinuous gold chain and elaborate letters carved or engraved on the case—I could make out an M but nothing else in all the curlicues.

"It really is a beautiful thing," said Maggie.

Len took it from me and carefully thumbed open the case. A plain white dial with the thinnest black hands, shaped like old axe blades and with delicately curved arrows at the tips, finely drawn Roman numerals round the edge. The rest of it was just plain, smooth, lustrous deep gold. So simple, plain and simple and beautiful.

"Now look at this," said Len. With the small blade of his pocket knife, he gently popped another groove and there were the workings of it, an exquisite nest of half circles and gears and cogs and teeth, and the maker's name in deep script engraved.

"Does it still work?" I asked.

"Nope," said Len. "It stopped years ago, oh, gee, when your dad was still a kid, I think. I was always afraid to wind it up or mess with it, didn't want to wreck it. But it's still such a nice thing to have, over all these years and years." He hefted it softly in his hand.

And I thought, suddenly and with sadness, that Len didn't have a son to give it to. Maybe he thought he would someday, but life didn't turn out like that. Or even a younger brother any more. But I realized that I couldn't see my dad even wanting it. Daddy was into new, the newest, "top of the line." New cars every other year, custom-made clothes just for him, and Mom had redecorated the condo twice already. This old house, this old watch, the old barn and trees . . . they had a history in them. And wasn't that worth something? Sometimes you had to rip out an old fence and build a new one, but some things could last.

"Can I take some pictures of it?" I asked. "It's so handsome . . ." For a minute I felt like I was going to cry.

"Oh, what a good idea!" said Maggie.

"Sure," said Len. "Don't lose it, though."

I flushed.

"I won't, I promise. And I won't wear it to build a fence, either."

Chapter 12

Travis called so early in the morning I wasn't up yet. Maggie just said he'd called and gave me the number.

"Umm, hi. Travis? It's Katie . . . Katie Myrdal?"

"Yeah, hey," he said. "Listen, I'm working this afternoon but gotta run a couple errands in town this morning . . . I wondered . . . I thought maybe you and I, we could go get some breakfast and then stop in at Marla's, the jewelry place? And see if she'd look at your watchband? Since I'm going into town anyhow . . . Sorry, is this too early?"

"No, no, it's fine . . . I need to, like, get ready, you know . . .?"

"An hour okay?"

"Umm, yeah, sure, that's good."

"Okay, see you."

Call ended. Well, we had each other's cellphone numbers now. I saved his.

I waved to Maggie, who was bent over doing something sweaty and violent to the vegetable garden, as I clambered up into Travis Gibb's truck. I picked up a couple DVDs plastered with library stickers from the seat as I buckled in.

"Oh, look, *Oliver*! My parents took me to see that in Chicago when I was a kid. I about wore out the CD," I said. "And *Music Man* . . ."

"My mom," said Travis. "She's crazy for old musicals. We get 'em from the library; probably seen every one they have. I know half of them by heart by now."

He glanced over at me as I warbled, "*There were birds . . . on the hill . . .*"

He smiled a little. "It's bells on the hill," he said. "Birds in the sky."

"Whatever," I said. "A couple years, we got series tickets to the Broadway in Chicago shows. It was fun . . . big, fancy, full-blown shows . . ." And apricot preserves in Paris. "Your mom would love it," I added lamely.

"She sure would," Travis said softly. "Jackrabbit!" He pointed.

Tall, lanky, the color of sand with ears like huge wooden spoons, the rabbit hulked at the gravel shoulder, then turned and bounded across the shortgrass field.

"Cool," I said.

"Not your regular old cottontail bunny, are they?" Travis said.

"That's for sure." Pause. "So . . . what's for breakfast?" There was an Applebee's and a Perkins on the highway . . .

"Nothin' special, just a little diner in town, Ginny's place. It's right across from Marla's."

"Sounds good," I said. "Thanks for doing this, by the way."

"Sure. Okay."

A truck approached from the other way; both the driver and Travis raised a forefinger off the steering wheel as they passed. The same thing happened when a dusty SUV came by.

"Everybody seems to know each other out here, don't they?" I said.

"Naw," said Travis. "We just all do that."

Half a dozen old guys in jeans and baseball caps with coffee mugs sat around one long table in the diner. They all looked up when we walked in, nodded or lifted a hand to Travis, and returned to their talk about nitrogen content and herbicides. Travis actually laughed.

"That's their lawns they're talking about," he said. "Just in case you think they're talking about their crops or something."

"Well, I wouldn't know anyway," I said. "I live in a high-rise."

It was a bright, cute place with blue checkered wallpaper borders spangled with sunflowers. The sun winked off the bumpers of the trucks parked outside the plate-glass front window. We slid into a booth.

The waitress came over, a thin, tired-looking middle-aged woman. When she smiled at Travis, her crooked front teeth showed.

"Hey, sweetie," she said. "Dougie get off okay this morning?"

"Yeah," he said. "Once I got him out of bed, he couldn't wait to get going. He's going fishing today with his buddy," he explained to me.

"And you must be Katie," she said, sticking out a hand to me. "I'm Joan. Welcome to the Opulence Café."

"That would be me," I said, shaking her hand. "Nice to meet you."

"You too. The usual for you, mister?" she said to Travis.

"Yup."

I was still looking at the menu, with little handwritten address labels stuck on where the prices had changed.

"The Sunrise Skillet is always good," he told me. "Or the biscuits and gravy."

"Okay, I'll do the skillet," I said. "Eggs, umm, over easy, I guess."

"Biscuit or toast?"

"Biscuit!" whispered Travis loudly. "She makes 'em herself."

"I do not," Joan rapped back. "But they are good. Ham, sausage, or bacon?"

"Ham," I said. "And biscuit. Thank you." Joan went off.

"Good choice," said Travis. "They keep the pigs out back and kill them to order." Then he sat back in the chair and enjoyed watching my face fall. But I didn't really believe him. Not for sure.

He was kind of a weird guy. Serious, silent. Then there'd be this odd little flash of humor, or a kind of inside chuckle, and then it vanished again.

The food was outstanding. It all came served in its own little skillet pan. The eggs weren't as good as *my* chickens' eggs, of course, but everything else was great. The hash browns were to die for. My mother would have just fainted to see me put it away.

Joan topped up our coffee. "Anything else for you?"

"No, thanks. I'm done!"

"On your tab?" she asked Travis. He looked down at the tabletop.

"Yeah, I guess," he said. "Excuse me, be right back." He got up and headed for the restrooms.

"I have a question," I said to Joan.

"Sure. Ask."

"You don't really keep the pigs out back, do you? For the ham . . . and bacon . . ."

She jerked her chin in the direction of the bathrooms. "He tell you that?"

I nodded.

"'Course not." She chuckled. "We do get most of it from a local guy. He raises his hogs the old-fashioned way, in a big old pasture with mudholes and grass. They have great lives, up till the very last day. And they taste like it." She paused. "Really nice to meet you, Katie. I know . . . I hear you've been through a bad time." She glanced again toward the restroom. "So has Travis. He's been kind of . . . kind of derailed since the fire and all. He doesn't quite know what to do with himself now . . ." The restroom door opened, and Travis was coming back.

"Anyway," she said. "You go on and have a good day now."

"Thanks," I said. "You too."

I stuck a five under the salt shaker before we left.

My high-top sneakers sank deep into the royal blue carpet in the jewelry store. Some kind of shimmery violin music played softly. A woman stood very erect behind the gleaming glass case at the back, in a royal blue pantsuit, her hair frozen and lacquered into a French twist.

"Good morning," she said in a rich, formal voice. She spoke like she was auditioning for *Downton Abbey*. "Welcome to Opulent Jewelers. How may I help you this morning?"

"Hi, Marla," said Travis. "How're you doing?"

"Very well, thank you," she replied smoothly. "A pleasure to see you, Travis. I hope you are well . . . well enough. I was so sorry to hear about the fire . . . and your loss. My condolences."

"Thanks, Marla. This is my friend, Katie Myrdal."

I smiled and was tempted, just for a second, to curtsey. But this woman was so serious, it would have been rude. Mean, even.

"Katie has a watchband . . . the clasp on it is busted. Could you have a look at it?"

"Of course," said Marla. "Let me see."

I dug the watch out of my jeans pocket and handed it over. She flipped it over, looked at it, then raised her eyebrows at me above the big plastic frames of her glasses.

"Very nice," she said.

"The clasp just won't quite catch," I said. She handled it delicately with her pink frosted nails, pinching and pushing.

"Hm. You're right, something isn't quite lined up there," she said. "But I expect we can straighten it out for you. If you'd like to come back in a couple of days . . .?"

"Sure, that'd be fine," I said. "No hurry or anything."

"Of course. Now, is there anything else I can show you today?"

A sudden impulse: "Can you fix other kinds of watches?" I asked.

"We do," she said. "What did you have in mind?"

"My uncle Len, he's got this amazing old gold pocket watch. From the Civil War, he said, but it stopped running years ago. Could you fix something like that?"

"Oh, dear. No, we really couldn't manage an antique like that. But you know what?" She looked brightly at me, like the idea interested her, and she started to talk more like a regular person. "Let me make some calls. There was a guy in Salina who was really good with those old watches. He might enjoy just having a look at it, anyway. I'll let you know if I find out anything."

"That'd be great," I said, and added to Travis: "Wouldn't it be cool if I could get that working again for Len?"

"Yeah, that'd be really nice," he said.

"Katie, what month were you born?" Marla asked me.

"September," I said, surprised.

"Ah, sapphire." She eyed me again, me in one of Daddy's old polo shirts and jeans. "I have some lovely little post earrings that would look darling." She slid open the back and reached inside. Then she glanced up at Travis and murmured, "Or a ring, perhaps?"

Travis resolutely gazed at the wall.

"Umm, no, thank you," I said hurriedly. "Just the watchband. We have to get going . . ."

"Of course," she said again, straightening up. "Give me a call in a couple of days about your band. I'm sure we can fix that."

"Thanks, Marla," said Travis. "I thought you might be able to help."

"Give my best to your mother," Marla said as he turned. "I see her over at Ginny's now and then. They keep her busy over there, don't they?"

I saw the skin of Travis's neck and face flush to the raw reddish color of the scars.

"Yes," he said through tight jaws. "Thanks a lot, Marla." And he steamed out the door, with me trailing behind him in a whirl.

He threw himself into the truck and slammed the door. I waited quietly on the other side till he took a few deep breaths, then yanked up the door lock. We just sat there for a minute.

"That was your mom, Joan, the waitress," I said, as calmly as I could. "Why wouldn't you have *told* me that?"

He didn't answer, staring out the windshield, thumbs flicking nervily on the steering wheel.

"I mean, really? You couldn't have told me she was your mom? You take me to breakfast there, and she's the waitress, and you introduce us but just kind of leave out that little detail? What was *that* about?" I was mad now. Confused, too. And like he'd played some kind of trick on me. "It's like you're . . . you're ashamed of her or something?"

"No way," he snapped. "Not ever. Not in ten million years. Don't you even think it."

"Then what? Did you think I was too high and mighty to associate with a mere waitress?" My voice got high and snarky. "If you're not embarrassed about her, then you must not think much of me! What did you even ask me here for, then?" I shoved open the truck door and launched myself out on the sidewalk. I stood there, arms wrapped tight around myself, near shivering. Now what? I'd have to call Maggie and make them come get me . . .

"Come back in the truck," said Travis. "Please, Katie, get back in the truck."

I did. Silently.

He sat, head bowed, still gripping the wheel.

"I'm sorry," he said. "I don't know. It just suddenly felt all weird. I just . . . I just wanted her to see you. To meet you, that's all. But then it got all messed up, like, oh look, Travis is bringing this girl home to meet his mother and all that, and it isn't like that. And by then it was too late and I didn't know how to fix it. So I just let it go. I saw the tip you left. It's twice what anyone would normally leave. And here you are, from this other world, like . . . big spenders, big tippers, and I'm like, what am I even doing?"

"My dad, he always tipped big. Part of it . . ." I started to puzzle it out. "Part of it was the show, I think. 'I'm a big shot, be nice to me, I'll be nice to you.' But once he said, even though he was kind of joking, that they had crappy jobs, having to be nice to jerks like him all the time. So they deserved every extra buck. So I figured she deserved the extra bucks. Even though we were pretty nice customers."

Travis tipped his head back and sighed.

"Ginny lets us eat there for free," he said. "Every little bit helps."

Christ. I was from a different world. Totally.

"Why is this town called Opulence?" I asked. "Because it doesn't seem very opulent to me. As hard as Marla tries."

Travis snorted. "That's a whole 'nother story. Look, I really am sorry."

"Please tell Joan . . . tell your mom . . . I really was glad to meet her. I liked her. And she told me they do *not* keep the pigs out back, but some local guy raises them."

"Yeah, that would be Bud Franklin. I can take you out there some time and you can see them yourself."

"If you do, I probably won't eat pork ever again. I've already kind of gone off chicken."

Travis started the truck.

"It's okay," I said. "I'm sorry too. Can I start my own tab at Ginny's now?"

"Only when Mom is working."

"Deal."

We dropped the DVDs in the library drop box and Travis took me home.

Maggie and I finished hoeing around the spinaches, and she showed me how to make a quiche for supper.

Chapter 13

Dee-dle dee-dle dee-dle dee-dle deee da da dee da da DEE . . .

Even in cellphone beeps, I still think that first part of Beethoven's "Für Elise" is so pretty. My mom says when I was really little, if I heard it, I'd swing my arms out and sway around the room to it. It was Mom's ring tone. We'd been texting and emailing here and there, but we hadn't actually talked in a while. I was out front, pulling weeds from around the irises, which was incredibly boring, but it was nice to stand up and see the irises looking like they were grateful. By the time I trotted over to the magic cellphone service spot by the mailbox, I could kind of decide how to sound when I picked up.

"Mom! Hi!" Cheerful. Pleasant.

"Hi, honey. It's mom," she said. Her voice sounded small.

"Yeah, hi. How are you? . . . How are you doing?"

"Oh, well . . . getting along. One day at a time, as they say." A little, brittle, phony chuckle. "So, what are you up to? How are . . . things?"

"Good. Yeah, good."

"What are you up to?" she said again. "I mean, are you finding enough to do or keep busy or what out there? Oh, I'm sorry, did I wake you up or anything?"

It was 10:00 AM!

"Oh, no, no, I've been up forever. I started getting up a lot earlier out here. Maybe it's the light or . . . whatever." But she was right. Back there, I usually stumbled out of my room closer to noon on weekends. But then I'd be up till all hours on the computer or fiddling with Photoshop or . . . or, I don't even know what I was doing. I kept talking: "It's really nice here. I don't know where the days go, you know? I take care of the chickens . . ."

"Really?" she said. "You take care of chickens?"

"Yep. I let them in and out and feed them and bring in the eggs. I know all their names now. I help Maggie with the garden, and she's been showing me how to cook, like omelets and quiches. And I helped build a new fence and . . . and, you know, just stuff like that." I trailed off. Apricots in Paris, only the other way around, sort of. "How are you doing? Are you okay?"

"I'm okay. Yeah, I'm working on it. I'm just really sick of talking to lawyers and police and accountants and not knowing what's going to happen next . . ." Her voice had a break in it, and she sounded really tired. Like she was about to cry.

Do parents know, I wonder, how scary it is for kids when their parents cry? All these years, they're the adults, they're in charge, they call all the shots, set all the rules, take care of all the bad stuff. Mommy and Daddy are the ones who keep you safe, help you when you're sick or hurt or scared. But if *they* cry, if *they're* scared or hurt and crying, then how can they take care of *us*? And all of a sudden, the world is really scary and you feel really alone. I couldn't say anything.

"But," she went on, like she was shaking it off, "but we do have some news. The lawyers have been all over it and talked to a judge, and they seem to think that it's okay about the condo. That it's in my name and it's mine, and since I didn't have anything to do with . . . with the business, then they aren't going to freeze it or take it away. So, at least there's a roof over our heads."

"Well, that's a good thing," I said.

"Yeah, well, that's the good news. I guess I wanted to tell you that even though they're not going to take it away, I don't think we can stay there. Long term, I mean. The taxes and mortgage and all, we can't keep it on our own. So I think we have to try to sell it and find somewhere else for us."

Silence. I thought about that and she waited to see what I would say.

"Okay," I said. "Not like I have a choice, but . . . it's okay."

"And," she said, with a sigh, "I'm thinking maybe not in the city, you know? Right in the middle of downtown. . . it was fine for a while, but it was your dad who was really into it and close to his offices and . . . but now . . . maybe in a quieter neighborhood. Or even in the suburbs somewhere, close to the train so we could get into town when we wanted to. But there's your school, too. You'd have to change schools, with the tuition and all . . . I guess overall now, we have to look at expenses, you know?"

"We have to retrench," I said solemnly. What book was that? In English lit . . . probably Jane Austen or Charles Dickens where everyone worried about their incomes and their fortunes, and money came and went like weather, and when it suddenly blew away, they'd talk about "retrenching."

"I get it, Mom. It's all different now." I looked up at the clouds, at the line of trees across the road, at the hawk sitting on top of the electrical pole. "It's fine. We'll retrench."

"The dealership gave me a pretty good offer on the . . . car. It's something. And I thought maybe I'd trade in the Escalade. It's so big, I always kind of thought I'd like a little Subaru, but your dad . . ."

"A blue one!" I said. "That would be so you."

She laughed a little down the line. "A blue Subaru, okay."

"Do you . . . do you want me to come home?" I asked. Not because I really wanted to, but because I thought I should ask.

"Are things okay there?"

"Yeah. Yeah, they are. I like it here. I'm good. And Maggie and Len are so nice. But . . ."

"I do miss you a little," Mom said. She sounded a little more like herself.

"Me too," I said. "I mean, I wish you were here too. It's really beautiful out here. But you'd have to wear boots. There's cow poop around."

Mom laughed again. "Okay, sweetie, I'll let you go tend to your poultry. Thank you . . . thank you for understanding. You're a good kid, you know?"

"Okay, Mom."

"I love you."

"Love you too."

Call ended.

The hawk lifted off and flapped away with a squeal. He took some of the ache out of my heart with him.

Chapter 14

My watchband was fixed. Maggie said they were going into town anyway the next morning—Len had an appointment—so we could just pick it up then. They trailed off to bed, and I was noodling on my laptop, hearing the murmur of Maggie's voice through the wall. Maggie was a talker, but at bedtime, sometimes I'd hear her go into a monologue, just murmuring on and on, and Len would occasionally say something brief or maybe laugh or chuckle a little. And after half an hour or so, they'd go silent.

I wasn't sleepy. I stood by the open window with my phone in my hand, and looked out at a sliver of silver moon in the scraggly tree limbs. I heard a long, soft, tootling fluty call—Maggie had told me it was a screech owl. They don't actually screech. I tapped up Travis's number and thumbed in: *Breakfast tomorrow, like 9? I'll buy if you drive me home after.* Was I asking a guy out? Maybe. I'd certainly never done that before. As soon as I hit Send, I wished I hadn't. I hoped his phone was off, so he wouldn't get the message till it was too late. Or maybe he'd be working and couldn't do it.

Ping.

I told Maggie and Len I was meeting him for breakfast when I was sitting in the back seat of the truck. I saw them glance at each other.

"And then we'll just get my watch and he'll drive me home," I said, talking too fast. "And then you guys can go do whatever you need and don't worry about me . . ."

"Okay . . ." Maggie said slowly.

"I met Joan," I said, "his mom, last time. She seems really nice. She'll probably be there and it's just right across the street . . ."

"Okay," said Maggie again. "Give me a call or a text when you're back, would you? We might run a couple errands too . . . do you want some more root beer?"

They had this fabulous root beer at the farm supply store. I loved that stuff.

"Oh, yes, please!" I said.

Len and Maggie looked at each other again.

Travis's truck was in front of the diner already and he was in the same booth. I had the skillet again, this time with bacon.

We ate, I paid—only fair, right? Not even fair, but at least . . .

"Come on this way," Travis said, turning away from his truck and toward the corner. I followed him around to an alley that went back up the block, behind the diner and the stores. He tugged open a back door and we were in a tiny vestibule, and off to the side, I could hear food sizzling and china clanking and rapid Spanish voices—Ginny's kitchen. Travis softly opened a peeling wooden door and motioned for me to follow. He groped for a switch, and a bare bulb lit up enough to make our way down some wooden stairs into the cellar. There were some boxes on shelves—extra kitchen stuff, canned goods, bales of paper towel and napkins—and a bare cement floor.

"Um, a basement?" I said. "You want me to take pictures of the diner basement?"

But actually, the light kind of trickled in through a tiny high window and made some shadows on the paper towel rolls, and I did take a couple shots. Sort of moody, film noir stuff—might look interesting in black and white.

"No, this is the cool part," said Travis. He opened yet another door, and we stepped across into another basement space. Big, cavernous, dusty, but lit by a bigger fan-shaped window. Walls of huge chiseled blocks of stone with ancient mortar crumbling out between them. Along the wall a heavy wooden . . . what? Shelf unit? With a counter in front, and a huge blotchy mirror . . . A bar! Like in the old Westerns—thick wood, with niches and shelves and a ledge for the cash register. Even a footrail, though it was bent and broken. One wooden stool in front of the bar, another one tipped over nearby.

"Oh my God," I breathed. "This is amazing. How old *is* this?"

"Maybe from cattle drive days. It was a speakeasy in Prohibition. These used to be the coal cellars, and then they put in gas lines, so they decided to use these tunnels for businesses. Look over here." He showed me a filthy alcove in the back corner, with no window light at all, with nothing in it but broken bricks, a lone broom worn down to nubs, and a rickety iron bedstead. "The barroom girls did their entertaining in here, they say."

I went behind the bar and started peering into the shelves and cupboards underneath.

"Careful where you put your hands," said Travis. "Snakes like to come down in here sometimes."

Before he finished saying the word "snakes," I slammed shut a door and jumped back. But at the back of one shelf, just catching a glint of light, I spotted one tiny dusty and crusted shot glass. It was stuck in the crackled varnish of the shelf, but with a tap it came loose. There was a dried brown ring in the bottom.

"Oh, look!" I held it out to Travis. "Look, some cowboy's last bit of whiskey, maybe! Still in the glass!"

I set it on the bar, where the light would just touch it, and took pictures, just the glass and the dust and the light. Travis murmured something.

"What?" I asked.

"Oh, nothing," he said, looking away. "Just an old song it made me think of . . . *Whack fol de daddyo, there's whiskey in the jar . . .*"

At least I think that's what the words were. But the thing was his voice: deep and soft and very . . . very musical, I guess.

There was another door, leading farther down the block. Travis gave a tug at a padlock on a crooked hasp.

"What's through there?" I asked. This was exciting! Another secret old room . . .

"Huh. Didn't used to be locked," he said, peering at the door jamb. "The theater is up above it."

"What theater? I didn't notice a theater on the block."

"Used to be," he said. "Way long ago, like 1870s, it was the opera house."

"An *opera house*? Seriously?"

He laughed. "This *is* Opulence, you know. How could they not have an opera house?"

"So what's the story there?" I said. "You said you'd tell me."

"This rich lord in England decided that he wanted to set up a town. You know how the oldest sons always inherited everything back then? Well, he thought there should be a place where those younger sons could emigrate to and make their own fortune and start farming. But there'd be this nice town with fine restaurants and theater and fox-hunting and all that so they could still live like 'gentlemen.' So he built Opulence and got some families to go in on it with him. I guess it lasted about five years, maybe. They hunted coyotes instead of foxes and the jackrabbits ate all their crops, and it was blazing hot in the summer and howling blizzards in the winter, and they decided they didn't really like it here. By then the cattle ranching business was taking over, and the town kind of just kept going along. The other side of the street burned down, oh, ages ago. They made the old opera house into a live theater and then a movie theater, but when everyone started going to the multiplex in Great Bend, they closed it down. Every so often somebody talks about trying to restore it and reopen it, but it never happens. They'll probably tear it down one of these days."

I sat on the stool in front of the bar, cradling the shot glass. I pictured grubby cowboys, painted girls in flouncy skirts, then maybe thin bobbed girls in fringy sheath dresses and rolled down stockings. Travis picked up the other stool, tested it carefully, then slid himself onto it and laid his elbows on the bar. I looked at him sideways, waggled the glass at him and said, "So, cowboy, how 'bout you buy me a drink?"

He rapped his knuckles on the bar and drawled, "Barkeep! A drink for the lady!" Then he stood up, walked around the bar and stood in front of me, straightening an imaginary bowtie.

"What'll it be, miss?" he said.

I held out the glass. "Same again. Whiskey. Neat." I tried for a sultry purr.

He mimed pouring into the glass. I tipped my head back and tossed it off, rapped the glass back down on the bar and went "Aaaaah!" like they do in beer commercials.

Travis leaned down, an elbow on the bar, and muttered in a confidential way: "Lady, if I was you, I wouldn't get mixed up with that one there." He jerked a thumb in the direction of the empty stool. "Comes from bad stock, he'll never amount to nothin'. Just sayin', you can do better than the likes of him."

My face felt hot. What the . . . but I carried on the game, whatever it was.

"Maybe I'll be the judge of that, mister," I sassed. "Besides . . . I don't think he even likes me."

"Ha," said the barkeep. "If he doesn't, he's crazy."

We looked at each other until we both looked away.

"Maybe we should go . . ." I said. "We better go get your watch," he said at the same time.

He waited in the truck while I went in to Marla's.

"Here you go," she said, offering the watch draped over her fingers. "It was a funny clasp. Not what we usually see on these. But it should be working now." She fastened it on me, I shook out my wrist and it stayed put. I paid her ten dollars.

"Oh, I almost forgot," she said. "I called the gentleman in Salina about your uncle's watch. He'll take a look at it if you get up that way." She handed me a card with a name and phone number scribbled on it.

"I could email him some pictures," I said.

She smiled at me and shook her head.

"I doubt Sherman does email," she said. "Give him a call."

"Thank you," I said.

"Is there anything else I can do for you today?" she asked. She was reverting to *Downton Abbey*.

"No, thanks, this is fine."

And I got back in the truck and Travis drove me home.

The red truck was in the drive. Len and Maggie had beat me home. Travis thanked me for breakfast, I thanked him for showing me the underground and told him I'd send him some pictures if they turned out okay.

"See you around," he said.

"Okay," I said.

As I went through the gate into the yard, he called something out the truck window to me as he started to back out. I think he said, "He does, you know."

So I felt kind of shaky and springy when I walked into the house. Len and Maggie were sitting silently in the living room. Maggie was crying.

Chapter 15

The feeling in the room zapped me straight back to the morning in the principal's office. I sat down in the nearest chair. This time I wasn't thinking it was about me, but that horrible sense that something really bad was about to happen was crawling all over me again.

I managed to say, "What's wrong?"

"It's Len," said Maggie, her voice raw. "Len's sick..." She kept swallowing and crying.

"I got prostate cancer," said Len.

No. No no no no no. It's not *fair*!

"Is it . . . is it bad?" I asked. Meaning, are you going to die?

"We don't know for sure yet," he said. "Not exactly how bad."

"He had a suspicious blood test," Maggie said. "So we saw that urologist in Wichita, and he said lots of things can make that test go up. So we'd do what he called 'watchful waiting,' and then do another test. Now it's even higher than before. And . . . and Doc Whiting here can feel . . . can feel . . . something, so he's pretty sure that's . . . what it is. And his back . . . sometimes it can spread to your bones and . . ." She was sobbing again. Len was sitting in his recliner, she was on the couch. I got up and went over and sat next to her.

75

"Maggie, honey," said Len from his chair. "We don't know that. My back's been trouble for years before this." He stared into his lap. "They're going to do a bunch more tests, an ultrasound, and a biopsy, or scans, and then we'll see."

"There might be surgery or radiation or . . . I don't know what all!" she cried.

"And we'll get through it," Len announced. "Whatever it is, we'll get through it." He stood up. "And the grass is still growing, so there's no reason I can't go mow the lawn."

"I can do it," Maggie and I both said at once. I'd never done it, but at the moment it seemed like the right thing to say. Len just got up, put on his hat, and went out. We heard the mower start up. We stood at the living room window and watched the green tractor roaring back and forth, back and forth, around the yard.

"I just thought," Maggie murmured brokenly, "I just thought there'd be more time. I mean, we met late and everything, but I just thought . . . we'd have more time."

That's the thing, isn't it. You never know when. You never know how much. One day, blam, it can all be over. And everything is different.

"And there still is," I tried to say. "You don't *know*, I mean, really *know*. There's things they can do. And it might be okay. Right? It might be okay? It's not like . . ." Not like a bullet in the head.

Maggie put her arms around me and we stood there in the bay window together, watching that green tractor still growling up and down, around and around. The air smelled sweet with cut grass. A wren chattered and warbled on the fence.

"I'm sorry we didn't get you any root beer today," said Maggie. I just hugged her.

I was going to call that guy in Salina and get that watch fixed.

Chapter 16

"Yalloo!"

**"Um, is this Mr. Olmitz? Sherman Ol-
mitz?"**

"Yes, ma'am."

"Um, hi, I got your name and number from Marla . . .
Marla in the jewelry place in Opulence?"

"Yes?"

He wasn't going to help this conversation along. Five
syllables in a whispery, thin little voice, like someone
who was a hundred years old.

"I'm . . . my name is Katie Myrdal and I have this
watch? It's my uncle's. He says it's from the Civil War,
and came down from his great grandfather and it doesn't
work and I was wondering if we could get it fixed? If
you'd look at it and see if you could? It's gold and really
nice and . . . I'd like to get it fixed for him." I took a
breath and almost launched into the whole story, the prostate cancer and everything, but stopped.

"You know the maker?"

"Umm, I can look . . ."

"Call me back and tell me what it says on the face."
Blip.

Okay then.

I got the watch out and called him back.

"It says E. Howard & Company."

Silence.

"Bring it in."

"Umm, when is a good time? And like, where are you?"

"Olmitz Watch Repair. Salina. Call the day before and say when. I'll look at it." Blip.

Thank God for Google Maps. I'd kind of gotten used to the idea that driving 20 miles to the grocery store, or 60 miles to get a watch fixed, was no big deal out here.

But I couldn't drive. Duh. And I really wanted to do this as a surprise. Maybe Travis . . . but those looks Maggie and Len gave each other when I said we were just having breakfast that morning . . . somehow I didn't think they were going to let me just take off with him for the day, with no explanation. It wasn't that they didn't like him, there was just something . . . I suppose they were *in loco parentis*, as they say (at school we put the emphasis on the *loco*), and here's this fifteen-year-old they're responsible for, and should they let me (gasp) DATE, and they'd probably want to call my mom, and . . . Okay. Maggie was going to have to be in on it. But maybe Travis could come too. Chaperoned, and all. I headed downstairs.

Maggie was making bread. The window over the sink was open and the sun was streaming in, lighting up her hands in the bowl of dough. I got my camera from the sideboard in the dining room.

"Don't mind me," I said. "Can I take some?"

She smiled and shrugged. "Go ahead. Should I hold still?"

"Nope, just keep doing what you're doing."

I crept and crouched and leaned around her and closed

in on her hands, on the shadows between her fingers and the shaggy dough clumps and the sun on her wrists. I'd never tried anything like this before. We'd see.

I straightened up.

"What's Salina like?" I asked.

"Salina? You want to go there?"

"I don't know, maybe . . ."

"Just a town," she said. "It's pretty big, actually—maybe 45-50 thousand people. Got a big movie complex, shopping malls, an arts center . . . Why?"

"I was talking to Marla at the jewelry store. She said there's a guy there who works on old antique watches. So I called him up. He said he'd look at Len's watch if I wanted. I want to see if we can fix it, fix the watch, for Len. Don't tell him! I want to do it for a surprise. Can you . . . would you take me up there some time? Without Len going?"

She stood there, peeling the clotted dough off her fingers. Her eyes got swimmy and she said, "Katie, that is so sweet. What a nice thing to think of . . ." She thought for a moment.

"Len hates shopping," she said. "They've got a Target up there, and a really great chicken restaurant. What if I tell him we want to go up and go shopping, stock up on some stuff besides Walmart." She made a face. "We could get ourselves a dinner and try this watch guy. I'm just thinking . . . to fix a watch like that might cost a lot. I don't know . . ."

"It's okay, really, I can do it, I want to! My dad gave me a credit card once, for emergencies, you know? I've never used it. And now . . . seems like as good a use as any. Better. Oh, let's do it, Maggie! And I wonder . . ."

"What, hon?" She turned the dough out onto a board and started kneading.

"Maybe I could see if Travis wanted to come? Just, just for fun?"

She stopped kneading "Katie. Travis is a good kid, he really is. But we're kind of responsible for you . . ."

I knew it.

"Have you mentioned him to your mom at all?"

I looked at the floor. "Umm, not really."

"Any reason?"

"Not really," I said again. "I've just . . . just not had a guy friend like this before. My dad, he'd probably joke about having him background checked, and going with us on every date till I was thirty, but my mom, I don't know . . ." I looked up at her. "But you'd be with us. Just going out for errands and chicken dinner, you know, just friends. It's not a *date* or anything."

She started kneading again.

"Okay," she said. "Call him up. We'll make a day of it. I'm pretty sure Len would be just as happy to stay home and watch a ball game on TV."

I texted Travis.

> **K** Call me when you have a sec?
>
> At work - you ok?
>
> **K** Mostly - sort of - will tell you later
>
> Ok

He called an hour later. It was hot out by the mailbox. A breeze scooped dust up off the gravel road but didn't cool anything off.

"What's up?" he asked.

"You doing anything Sunday afternoon?"

"No, not working or anything. Why?"

"You want to go to Salina with Maggie and me?"

"What's up?" he asked again.

"Remember I asked Marla about fixing Len's watch? I talked to the guy in Salina and he said to bring it in. So we're going to drive up there and run some errands and stuff, and eat a chicken dinner . . ."

"At the Cattleman Hotel? Oh, yeah, I'd go for that!"

"I guess that must be it, Maggie said it was good."

"The *best*!"

"And take the watch in . . . we want to surprise Len, so it's a secret. Because . . ." I swallowed. "Because we just found out he's sick."

"What's the matter?" He sounded suddenly tense.

"Prostate," I said slowly. "Prostate cancer, it looks like."

Silence.

"Oh, man. I am really sorry, Katie, truly sorry. That just sucks."

Silence at my end. I couldn't quite talk. "Yeah," I said finally. "It does. It really does. It's so . . ."

"So unfair," he snapped. "They're so good, such good people, such a good couple."

I was crying. Unfair. "Maggie said," I gulped, "Maggie said she just thought there'd be more *time* . . ."

"So you're going to try to give him some, in a way," said Travis.

"I don't know now. Maybe I should leave the watch stopped, not start it up again."

"Would it help?"

"'Course not," I answered. "I think he'd like to have it running. So I want to try."

There was a long pause. I scraped the toe of my sneaker in the dirt. I sniffed up snot and wiped my face.

"So do you want to come? At least you'll get a chicken dinner out of it."

"Yeah," he said. "I do want to come. What time?"

"Noon or so. I think Maggie wants to go to church first. I'm . . . I may go with them. You want to meet us here or something?"

"That'll work," he said. "Katie?"

"Yeah?"

"I'd give you a hug if I was there. If you wanted me to, anyway."

"I'd take a hug," I said.

Chapter 17

Olmitz Watch Repair was down a narrow alleyway off the main street in Salina. We never would have found it except for a funny little painted sign of a clock face with the time showing three fifteen—both hands pointing with big arrows on the ends, down the alley. We shoved the door open (it stuck) and tripped into a linoleum-floored room with a couple of vinyl-seated chairs that looked like they had been rescued from a banquet hall. There was a counter and a work table set under the window that looked out into the alley. And a mountainously huge man in a wheelchair. I had pictured a little skinny guy, like Geppetto in Pinocchio or something, from that wheezy voice on the phone. But now I could see why he sounded that way: oxygen tubes from a tank bolted to his chair, making a little mechanical hiss and click. He looked swollen and soft and yellow.

"Hi," I said. "Mr. Olmitz?"

"Yes. You Katie? With the old watch?"

"Yes, this is my aunt Maggie and my friend Travis."

"Hi," said Maggie and Travis.

He nodded. "Heart failure," he said, pointing at the tank. "Let's see it."

I handed over the box. He switched on a lamp with a magnifying lens built into it, and popped the watch open easy as anything with fingers so thick I was amazed he could even bend them. We stood there, while he peered inside the watch and looked carefully at the face of it. There were racks of all kinds of little pointy tools and pliers and tweezers, all very neat and orderly. It smelled like metal and oil and cleaning fluid. There was no dust anywhere. I wondered how he kept it so perfectly clean like that.

"This is a lovely old watch," he said. "I think I can get it running again. Couple weeks okay? If any of the gears need work, it might take longer, but from what I can see, it looks pretty good."

It was the longest speech I'd heard him make, and he was breathing hard at the end of it. He sat with his head back for few moments to recover. I don't exactly mean lucky, but it seemed good that he had a job he could keep on doing in a wheelchair, on oxygen, quietly by himself.

"Sure, yeah," I said. "However long . . . no hurry. Do you want, like, a deposit?" He smiled, the corners of his mouth kind of disappearing into his cheeks, and made a sound like he meant to laugh or chuckle.

"I got your watch," he said. "Worth a lot more to me to sell off again than it'll cost to fix it."

"Really?" said Maggie. "It's valuable, then?"

Olmitz nodded. "In original shape like this, a couple thousand."

"Oh my!" said Maggie. "To think we've just had it in the dresser drawer . . ."

"Good a place as any," he said.

Travis had been standing quietly, just waiting around.

"How's business?" he said, just to be polite.

Olmitz shrugged. "Not great," he said. "Don't get many jobs like this. Mostly just batteries, replacement bands . . . cheap watches these days, not worth fixing. Sometimes someone has one of those knockoffs like yours," he nodded at me, "and I clean those up for them if they want. Not many of the real thing around here."

Maggie and Travis were looking at me.

"Excuse me?" I said. "A knockoff? My watch?"

He held out his hand. I pulled the watch off and dropped it into his doughy palm.

"You had trouble with the clasp?"

I nodded. "Marla said something about how the clasp was different from what they expected . . ."

He nodded. "First sign." He flipped the watch over and showed me the back of it. The Rolex name and the little crown logo. "Real Rolexes have plain backs. Never engraved. Only engraved inside the bracelet, here . . ." He pointed. "Lettering looks rough, not evenly spaced. If I had a real one here, I'd weigh them—this one would be lighter. The diamonds are . . ."

"Not real," I said. "Right?"

"Right," he said. "Have to look with a jeweler's loupe, but . . . pretty good, but not the real thing."

"But how did you know?" Travis broke in. "You couldn't see any of that engraving and stuff with her wearing it!"

"You garden?" Olmitz asked.

"I do," said Maggie.

"In spring, when the shoots are just coming in, how do you know a weed from a flower?"

"I just . . . I just do," Maggie said slowly. "Just years of looking at them, I know which is which."

Olmitz shrugged. "Yep."

And there I stood, with that goddamned watch in my

hand, with a wail inside my head: "*Did Daddy know?*"
Did Daddy get ripped off too? Mr. High-Powered King of
the World Business Genius, did some scuzzbag or some
swanky-looking website fool him? Or did he *know* he
was buying a fake, and just figured I'd never know . . .
and I remembered him grinning and saying what a "great
deal" he got on it. He was a fraud, a phony—gypping his
daughter on the sly, or thinking he was smarter than anyone else when he wasn't. Or both.

I walked out. I guess Maggie and Travis completed the
business with Olmitz, and they found me braced against
the wall of the alley.

"Damn him!" I croaked through clenched teeth. "I
can't believe he . . . God*damn* him anyway!" And Travis
put his arms around me and I cried on his chest.

"I know," he said. "I know. They can be sons of bitches."

"But I didn't *know*!" I cried.

"Maybe better that way," he said. "And this, oh, Katie,
it's just a watch, really."

"It's not just the watch," I snuffled. "It's *him* I didn't
know . . . nobody did! Look what he's *done* to people!"

"I know," he said again. And hugged me very tight for
a minute. I pulled away and turned to face Maggie, standing sadly in the alley.

"At least we know Len's watch is for real. And it
means something!" I said.

"Yes," she said, hugging me. "It absolutely does."

Chapter 18

We scuffed up the street. It was hot. We weren't saying much. We passed a large window, some kind of gallery it looked like. Travis glanced in, then stopped.

"Wait," he said. "Want to have a look?"

KScapes, said a poster in the window. Kansas photographers and landscape. I shrugged.

"Okay," I said. "If you want. Do we have time?" I asked Maggie.

"Sure, let's," she said.

Just one room, with maybe three dozen pictures, half a dozen photographers. A girl at a desk smiled and said, "Hey," when we came in. "Enjoy," she added.

Sunsets. Sunsets were definitely a *thing*. Huge format, lurid, Photoshopped with extra pink and purple, like Hallmark calendars. They made me depressed. Obviously my little project had been done by everyone in the state who had a camera. And clouds. Towering clouds, shelf clouds, storm clouds, several lightning bolts over silos. Travis was over on the other side of the room, looking hard, reading labels.

"Katie!" he said. "Come see these. I *know* this guy!"

A silvery figure rising out of sodden leaves. A sleek curve of chrome across a ghostly pitted green surface. A sorrowful old car with one headlight hanging like a loose eyeball. A swatch of golden grass framing a . . . a . . . I don't know what it was, some hefty metal mechanical thing. They were *my* kind of pictures: details, shapes, colors.

"It's Nemo's junkyard!" Travis said.

I had no clue what he was talking about. "Out west of town, on the highway," he explained. "I've been there a bunch of times—my dad would go there and get parts for his junkers. The guy who took these pictures . . . it's Nemo! I had no idea . . . Wow."

They were terrific pictures. The color was gorgeous, rich but muted. Perfect focus—except when he wanted it to be soft. And a little mysterious: what *was* that? A hood ornament. A bit of trim. Part of a wheel. They just made a design all their own. Out of a junkyard.

"Who knew?" Travis kept saying. "Old Nemo, who knew he took pictures like this? All these years, just Nemo the junkyard guy."

And the labels on the wall just said, "John Nemos, Opulence."

I think we all felt a little better.

We went to Target and bought stuff. They had Wrangler jeans on sale, and Travis bought a couple pairs for himself and his little brother. I bought a pretty blue glass pie dish for Maggie . . . I dropped and broke one of hers when I was putting it away the week before. I felt bad, but she said not to worry, it was one she'd gotten for two bucks at Goodwill, so it wasn't some priceless heirloom. Maggie was thrilled to find some halfway decent wooden clothespins—all the Walmart had were crappy plastic ones that fell apart. Milano chocolate orange cookies—we ate the whole bag while we were still shopping, and

Maggie said it was okay, they'd just ring up the empty bag when we checked out. And I got myself a $27.99 Timex Expedition watch. I put it on in the parking lot, raised my fist in a sort of salute and shouted, "Time marches on!"

And even after the Milano cookies, when we sat down in the swirly-carpeted dining room of the Cattleman Hotel, the smell of the chicken made us practically drool.

People lined up at the buffet armed with thick white plates and napkin-wrapped silverware clutched in their fists. Fried chicken and dressing, meat loaf and mashed potatoes, biscuits, peas, green beans, corn, coleslaw, creamed spinach . . . it smelled like heaven. And angel food cake and strawberries. We hardly even talked that much. We ate. I had like four drumsticks.

"Told you this was the best," said Travis, shoving back from the table and neatly stacking up the several plates he'd accumulated. I nodded, trying to tongue strawberry seeds out of my molars.

Maggie wiped her mouth and said, "I wish Len was here." She looked at me. "No, hon, it's okay, we did this for a reason. But next time . . ."

"Absolutely!" I said. "Can we bring him anything?"

"It's a buffet," said Maggie. "I don't think they let you have doggy bags."

Travis got up and walked over to the cash register, where a girl about my age was ringing people up as they left. He smiled at her and started talking to her. She beamed and smiled right back, and an alarm started whining in my head.

Wait! Isn't she grossed out by his scars? His deformed hand and that gnarly ear? I'm his friend, I'm the one who doesn't even notice those things any more . . . *she* should be more, oh, I don't know, kind of cautious about it, right off the bat, instead of talking and smiling and glancing around in that sly way, and handing him a big Styrofoam clamshell box.

Travis slipped a bill out of his wallet and gave it to her, she scribbled up a bill. He got back into line and loaded up that box with chicken and potatoes and corn and a biscuit, and wedged in a brownie at the end. He tiptoed back to us in this exaggerated way, slid the box onto the chair next to Maggie and said, "You just have to ask the right people." She stood up and kissed him. He sat back down, and I felt his hand under the table, reaching for me. I took it and we just sat there, not saying anything. Not even looking at each other, except maybe stealing a glance when the other wasn't looking. Just sat there, holding hands under the table.

What a good guy, I thought. A good person. And I started to hope, really hope, that he liked me, because I sure was getting to like him. A lot.

Funny how not saying anything can be sad, or tense, or preoccupied—and sometimes it's just being happy and not needing to. Not right that moment, anyway.

Chapter 19

This may sound weird, but I had never actually been inside a hospital before we took Len up to Kansas City (the Kansas side) for his surgery. He'd had a bunch of blood tests and scans and a biopsy at the hospital in Great Bend. It was prostate cancer, but they said it looked like it was "contained" inside the gland, and not a very high score, which is supposed to be good. So they said if he had it surgically removed, that might just take care of it. The university had a robot that was supposed to make the surgery a little easier. They even met the surgeon on a web conference call—Len was kind of impressed that he could sit there in the doctor's office in Opulence and talk to the surgeon on the computer, like he was sitting in the same room with her. Maggie chuckled and said, "So he found out what Skype is."

We had this kind of fraught discussion about logistics. It was a three-and-a-half-hour drive, so they had to drive over the night before, and he'd stay at least one night in the hospital.

"So that's going to be two nights in a motel," said Maggie. "And maybe three. It's going be a drag for you . . ." I was kind of hurt.

"Well, I can just stay here if you want."

"Three nights on your own out here? I don't know . . ."

"Then I'll come. I'd rather come with you."

"It'll be a lot of hours with nothing to do, and I'll be a wreck . . ."

"Then I'll keep you company, unless you'd rather I stayed here and not be in the way. But it's not like I need a baby-sitter!"

"No, no, I know, I just don't know what's best . . ."

"Wait! What if Travis . . . and his mom and his brother . . . came out and stayed here with me?"

"Oh, no, I don't think so . . . she works some nights and you'd still be here by yourself with . . ."

That was it. Okay. What would the kids get up to on their own . . .

"Then I'm coming with," I said. "I'll bring a book, I'll bring my iPad." I grabbed it off the table next to me and flipped it open. Googled up KU hospital, info for visitors . . . yep. Wireless. "We're good. I'm coming."

"Good," said Len.

We took I-70 across—the speed limit is 75, and everyone drove 80 . . . but everyone drives 80 in Illinois, and the speed limit is 55. Go figure. I sat in the back seat behind Maggie with a book (Maggie had turned me on to these Icelandic murder mysteries, and the minute she'd finished this one I grabbed it and wouldn't let her tell me anything about it), but couldn't stop looking out the window. Lots of people wouldn't believe me, but the Flint Hills were just amazingly beautiful. Like what we drove through the day I got there, only grander—rolling hills and mesas and long expanses of green like a pool table, and those piled up clouds in a sky that never stopped changing. Like some of those photographs in the gallery. Maybe you had to be from here to get pictures like that.

We went by a huge military base, with black helicopters like monster dragonflies tethered to the asphalt, and giant buildings and hundreds of cars and trucks and jeeps, and not a single human being to be seen. It was a little creepy. Billboards for gun shops and what they called "gentleman's clubs" (yeah, right) and a nasty one of Obama painted up to look like the Joker from the Batman movies. Once we got to Topeka, it was just like any other city expressway, but without traffic jams. Maggie started getting nervous when we got into Kansas City, so I sat up and read signs and helped navigate. It felt a little weird, being back in a big city. I guess I'm used to it, but I could kind of see how it might look to someone who wasn't. Someone cut us off in front of an exit ramp and I muttered, "What a dickhead!" I thought Maggie would choke laughing, and we almost missed our own exit.

But we got there, to the Holiday Inn a couple blocks from the hospital. They'd messed up the reservation, and didn't have the room Maggie had asked for, with two queen beds. But then I told the clerk we were there for cancer surgery at the hospital, he was really nice and gave us a suite for the same price—one bedroom with a king bed and I could sleep on the sofa bed in the living room part. Maybe I had learned something useful from my dad, besides how to talk at stupid drivers.

Like I said, I had never been in a hospital before. When we walked in the main lobby the next morning, it looked like a fancier version of the downtown Holiday Inn. But I had been in a few fancy hotels, and it felt different, sounded different, smelled different. Everything was hard, everything was polished, everything was cleanable and sanitizable, and absolutely nothing was comfortable or soft. Hard-soled footsteps clacked, voices echoed, overhead announcements blared. The enormous flower arrangements were all fake, even the marble-looking floor tiles were fake—I could tell because I could see the same exact patterns in the swirls in every tile on the elevator floor. Maggie and Len never let go of each other's hands. I don't know who looked whiter in the face when a really sweet, cheerful nurse rolled Len off to the holding area, Len or Maggie. She kissed his cheek, he touched her face, and she and I wandered out to the waiting room to, well, wait.

I found the cafeteria. The coffee was terrible. M&Ms cost $1.50 in the vending machine, which was out of order. I brought tea back to Maggie, but she didn't drink it. I emailed my mom. I texted Travis. He had sent a nice text the day before, telling me to wish Len good luck. I tried to read. I wandered around. Maggie sat. It took almost exactly as long as it took us to drive from Opulence to Kansas City. Maggie didn't even recognize the surgeon at first when she came out in her bulbous paper bonnet and bright pink Croc shoes.

"He did awesome!" said the surgeon. "All done, all gone. I sampled a few lymph nodes, and the touch prep looked clean on all of them; we'll get a final report tomorrow. You can meet him up in his room; they're moving him up there now. He'll be groggy, but we started the pain meds already, so he shouldn't feel too bad."

"So," said Maggie slowly, "he'll be okay? You think he'll be okay?" The surgeon smiled and patted her shoulder.

"Let's just say that whatever he eventually dies of, it probably won't be this. So go on, go on up to 5th floor, room 5103."

"5103? That's our home address number," Maggie said. "That must be a good omen, don't you think? Thank you! Thank you, Doctor . . . Doctor . . . I'm sorry, I don't remember your name!"

"Kumar," said the young surgeon. "No worries. I'll be by later to see you all." And she clomped off through the doors behind her.

Maggie looked vaguely around her. I picked up the big plastic bag of Len's clothes. He'd looked so odd in the brand new sweatpants and brilliant white sneakers he'd worn to the hospital, but they'd told him to dress in loose, easy clothes. I'd never seen him in anything but work boots and jeans, not once. I gathered up my bag and Maggie's purse, and suddenly she kind of came to, and said, "Which way is the elevator?"

And off we went.

Chapter 20

Len looked old, groggy, and gray against the white pillows. Maggie leaned down to kiss him, and he gazed at her stupidly at first, then he smiled a little.

"How you feeling?" she asked him.

"Like I had a few holes punched in me," he said. "And a chunk missing."

"Sounds about right," she said.

"You know, I only did this because of you," he said. "You seemed to want me around a while longer."

"You bet," Maggie said brightly. Then she blew her nose. "The doctor said you did great. It's all gone, she thinks."

"Really?" He was staring at the bedspread with this thoughtful look on his face. "So you are stuck with me for longer." He looked up at her. "Good. I'm glad about that."

That's just how they were with each other.

A nurse bustled in, and there was a lot of chat about pain meds and nausea and IV lines and how to work the TV. Len drifted off to sleep, and we went back down to the cafeteria. I warned Maggie off the coffee, but the bean and chard soup wasn't bad at all, and the peanut butter cookies were homemade and warm.

By evening, they had him sitting up and dangling his feet—so weird to see Len even had bare feet—at the edge of the bed. He was tired, but not hurting that much. Maggie sat in the big chair and watched the news; I stretched out on the vinyl couch and read my book. My phone chimed—Travis texting to see how Len was. We messaged back and forth a few times.

Beethoven from my phone . . . my mom.

"How did it go with Len?" she asked. "How's he doing? I've been thinking of him and you all today, since you emailed this morning."

"Pretty good, I think," I said. "They said it's all taken out and he should be okay. I'm . . . we're . . . really glad."

"Where are you?"

"We're just hanging out at the hospital for a while . . ."

"Is Maggie there? Can I talk to her?"

I handed off, and Maggie talked to my mom for a few minutes. It was nice of her to call. My mom . . . well, she knew how to do the social graces thing. But it's not like she was close to Maggie and Len. Of course, I hadn't even heard of them before . . . before my dad happened. And now look. Here we were.

Maggie gave me back my phone. She looked happy.

"Hey," my mom said. "I think I have some news."

"You think?"

"Well, it's not for sure, but . . . I think I might have a job."

A job? My mother? Seriously?

"A job?" I said. "Like, what?"

"At the arts college . . . I helped out with some fund raising for them last year, remember?"

"Oh, yeah, I remember." One of her "Friends of" kind of deals.

"They've got someone in their marketing office who's going out on maternity leave in September, and through

98

the grapevine, you know . . . anyway, they wondered if I could fill in while she's gone."

"Doing what kind of stuff?" I just couldn't imagine my mom working. In an office, or whatever. She seemed like such a purely recreational sort of person.

"Oh, helping write press releases and organizing meetings or events, that kind of stuff."

She sounded almost excited about it, but I just couldn't quite picture it. Her voice got a little sharp on me: "I do have a degree in communications and public relations . . . I used to work, you know, before I met your dad."

"I guess I didn't really know," I said. "I never knew you working. That's great, Mom, really, it sounds like—what do they say—'a good fit'?"

She laughed then. "You got the lingo already," she said. "I think so, though. Let's face it, life is different now. Who knows what's going to happen, but I better get my act together. We've got some life to get through yet, you and me. You okay? Still feeding your chickens?"

"Yep," I said. "I'm worried about them with us gone a couple days, but the Kirchners down the road said they'd come up and look after them. They'll be mad at us, leaving them in the coop."

"Okay, well, I'll let you go. Oh, I talked to a realtor, and she's going to send me some info on houses, like we talked about? There's one in Western Springs that sounds kind of nice. I'll send you the listing, okay? Take care, honey—love you!" And she was gone.

I poked at my iPad. Western Springs lets you have four chickens.

I dozed off on the couch. When I came to a little while later, with my neck and shoulder all clinched up, it was to the murmur of Maggie's voice, like I heard her through the walls at night. It was pleasant to just lay there, sleepy and a little out of it, and listen to it. The room was dark except for a little light at Maggie's chair. Her voice trailed along, and occasionally Len would grunt a word or two. After sleeping most of the day, he must have been wakeful. As I listened, I realized Maggie wasn't just talking. She was reading. That's what she was doing in the night: she was reading to Len. It touched me—it seemed so old-fashioned, but so sweet and . . . and sort of intimate. Like maybe I shouldn't be listening? But I did. There was a woman named Bathsheba, and a man called Troy, who seemed to be bad news, and an angry character called Boldwood. It was like coming into a movie half way through, but it kind of caught me. Finally Maggie glanced up and saw me lying there with my eyes open. She laughed.

"You caught us!" she said. "Bedtime reading. Helps Len get to sleep, or at least gives him something to listen to while he's awake. He's quite an authority on Dickens now, and now we're doing Hardy." She held up the book: *Far From the Madding Crowd.* "The movie is pretty good too."

"Is it okay if I listen?" I asked. "Would you mind?"

"You might learn something, young lady," growled Len from his bed. "About good literature." Maggie laughed.

"We'll have to watch the movie so I can catch up," I said.

"But we'll have to stop it before you see how it ends."

"Deal."

"You want to go on back to the hotel?" Maggie asked. "I'll be along in a bit. You're okay walking back by yourself?"

I figured if I could take the train to school every day in Chicago, I could manage three blocks in Kansas City.

"Yeah, no problem. See you later."

I picked up my stuff. Maggie reached a hand out, pulled me down and kissed me good night. I bent down and kissed Len too. I'd never done that before. He made a funny puckered face and turned his cheek as though he was embarrassed, but somehow I knew he didn't mean it.

"Good night, grumpy puss," I said to him. "See you in the morning!"

Just as I was falling asleep in the sofa bed, my phone went.

"Kathy Myrdal?" A woman's voice.

"Katie Myrdal, yes . . ."

"I'm calling from Olmitz Watch Repair. We've got a watch here for you, you left to be fixed?"

"Yes! Is it done?"

"Yes, he finished it. Look, if you could pick it up in the next couple of days, that would be good." She sounded odd, and it was kind of strange to be calling at like eleven at night.

"Okay, we'll try . . . how much will it be?"

"Oh, um, I'm not sure, I'm not there right now . . ."

"Oh. Okay, well, we'll try to get there in the next couple of days."

"Thanks a lot," she said. And hung up.

As I lay back down, I tried to figure out how to pick it up, and decided we probably couldn't do it without Len knowing this time. Maybe we could even go through Salina on the way back? Well, Maggie and I would figure it out.

Chapter 21

"I know what!" Maggie announced as we rolled past the exit to Abilene. "Cozy burgers!"

Len looked sideways at her. "You want cozy burgers?"

"You up for a couple?" she asked. "We haven't had them in ages."

"What's a cozy burger?" I asked from the back seat.

"Ooooh, you'll see!" she said, grinning at me in the rear-view mirror. "We'll go home through Salina and pick up a sackful. Didn't you say there was something you needed to pick up in that shop downtown there anyway? It's like three blocks from there."

Maggie. She was good. I grinned back at her.

"Oh, yeah, that's right!" I chirped. "What a good idea."

"Okay," said Len. "They're pretty famous around here," he added over his shoulder to me.

They'd cut him loose from the hospital the very next afternoon, he was doing so well. Not that he would've complained no matter how bad he felt, but everything looked good, and he wanted to go home. I'd told Maggie about the call from the watch place while we were getting our stuff together at the hotel, and she'd promised to figure something out. Maybe we couldn't keep it secret from Len much longer, but we could at least get there and get it back.

The Cozy Inn was just . . . adorable. A little red and white corner place, a tiny diner with old wood cupboards, six stools and a line out the door. It smelled like White Castle, which my mom would never EVER let us go to. Grease and meat and onions . . .

"I'll wait in line," Maggie said, shooing me up the street. "Just come on back to the truck. You'll want at least two burgers, and I'm going to get some frozen ones too."

"Be five minutes!" I said, and rounded the corner at a jog.

I shouldered the sticky door open, out of breath. Only one chair on the linoleum. A woman in khaki cargo shorts and flipflops was smoking a cigarette at the workbench.

"Hi," I panted. "I'm Katie, to pick up the watch?"

She stood up and picked up the box.

"Good," she said. "Thanks for coming. We're trying to get things . . . things cleared up, and this was the last one left." I realized there was nothing at all in the place. The worktable was bare, nothing but the phone, a credit card swiper, and the coffee mug she was tapping her cigarette ash into.

"Did . . . has Mr. Olmitz, um, retired? I mean, I know he has heart problems . . ."

She looked blankly over my shoulder and rubbed her puffy eyes.

"Dad passed away last weekend," she said.

Oh, no.

"Oh, I'm so sorry, I didn't know . . . I'm so sorry."

When were people going to quit dying on me?

"Thank you." She was biting her lip. "He'd been sick a long time. They said it could be like this. He sat up,

103

coughed, and just . . . just went. He was gone before the paramedics got there."

"I'm sorry," I said again. What else was there to say? I'd met him once. *Why did he have to go die too?*

"But I have to tell you," the woman said, "he told us all about this watch of yours. He was so happy to have something this . . . elegant was the word he used . . . elegant to work on. He didn't get to see something like this very often. He said it was really beautiful and he was happy he could get it going again."

"It's for my uncle," I said. "He just got out of the hospital, and I wanted to get it fixed for him. It's been in his family for a long time. I'm glad . . . I'm glad your dad got something out of doing it for him. I wish I could tell him thank you from us."

She handed me the box. I opened it up and took the watch out. He'd polished it—it was silky and smooth and shone. He'd even polished the crystal—got most of the old scratches out, it was clear and sparkling. And it ticked. It showed 4:17 PM, and the slender second hand was stepping delicately round the dial. I held it up to my ear and it ticked, ticked, ticked.

"He said to just be careful to wind it regularly, but not too much. It should last another hundred years."

"Thank you," I said. "I'll tell him. How much . . . what do I owe you?"

"One fifty," she said. I fished the credit card out of a back slit in my wallet and gave it to her. She swiped and tapped, waited . . . "It's been declined," she said.

"What?"

"I'm sorry—it declined your card." She gave me the card. It wasn't expired, I'd never even used it! And then it hit me. Of course. It was in my dad's name. It had been frozen or cancelled so we couldn't run up bills and buy stuff while they were still figuring out how much my dad had stolen from people. "I can take a check . . .?"

I didn't have a checkbook. And I didn't have a hundred and fifty dollars in cash. I didn't know what to do. We'd have to come back, I'd have to ask Maggie . . . what was I going to do *now*?

Sherman Olmitz's daughter said, "Look, you know what? Just take it. You got a piece of paper?"

I dug mutely in my bag and came up with the receipt from Target for my Timex watch.

She pulled a pen from a box I hadn't noticed under the worktable and scribbled on it. "Here's my name and address. Take your watch, send me a check when you get home. I know my dad was happy to work on it, and that means a lot to us. I hope your uncle will be happy to get his watch back. And I . . . I guess we're done here." She stooped and picked up the box. Ranged inside it were the little racks of tiny tools—little pointy pliers, screwdrivers the size of toothpicks, tweezers. I imagined them in his swollen fingers, carefully, precisely fitting and unfitting the bits and pieces of Len's watch. And setting it going again.

"I will," I whispered. "Thank you. Take care. Thank you . . ."

And I left.

The truck cab was bursting with the hot burger smell.

"All set?" said Maggie cheerfully.

I nodded.

She handed me a grease-spotted bag, and looked at me carefully. "Everything okay?"

I nodded again. My mouth was full of warm meat and onion and I wasn't sure the lump closing my throat was going to let it go down.

"I'll show you when we get home," I mumbled.

She didn't say anything more, but kept an eye on me in the rear-view mirror the rest of the way.

Chapter 22

Len was pretty tired when we got home. We just dumped our bags in the dining room, Maggie put the box of burgers in the freezer, and Len shut himself in the bathroom.

"He's got a catheter in his bladder," Maggie murmured to me. "He's not happy about it, but he has to have it for a week until the swelling goes down inside."

I took my stuff upstairs, and when I came down, Len was still in there and Maggie was hovering outside.

"Len?" she said, tapping with her nails on the door. "Len?"

"What!" from inside.

"You okay in there?"

A sort of a growl.

"Len, is everything all right?"

"It's fine! I just . . . damn!"

"Do you need that handout the nurse gave you? I can get it for you. It's right here . . ."

"For Christ's sake, let me just do this!"

Maggie spun away from the door and leaned her hands on the kitchen sink. I went to look at the bird feeders outside the living room windows. I'd never heard him snap at her like that.

The toilet flushed and Len came out. He dropped into the recliner in the living room. I went upstairs again. When I heard them speaking, voices low and not angry, I came back down with the square white box in my hand.

"Sorry," he said to me. "That was not called for."

"I have something for you," I said. "Maybe this will cheer you up?"

He took the box, looking a little puzzled. The same old white box the watch had always been in. He opened it up and took up the watch.

"Listen," I said. He looked at it again, then held it up to his ear.

"It's going," he said.

I nodded and smiled at him, a smile that almost hurt me. "We got it fixed."

"*You* got it fixed," said Maggie. "She found out how and arranged it."

"There was a guy in Salina . . ." I began. Then I blurted out to Maggie: "Mr. Olmitz died last week. He fixed the watch and then he died, and he said it was so elegant and he was so glad to do it, and then my credit card was frozen and I didn't have the money and I couldn't pay her and . . . and . . ."

Len held out his hand to me. I gave him mine, and he closed it up in both of his big, dry, bony ones, like he had when we first met at Daddy's memorial service. The watch ticked between our palms.

"Don't worry," he said. "We will make it all right." He held my hand tight and murmured, "My poor Kate. My poor little Kate." And let me go.

Chapter 23

Friday night, Len went to bed early. He was tired, he felt cold even though it almost hit 100 degrees that day. In the morning, he muttered curses in the bathroom as he did whatever he was doing with that catheter. Then he let Maggie in the bathroom, and when they came out, he had a thermometer in his mouth.

Maggie called the doctor. "His temp is 101.5, and one of those incisions looks red and puffy . . . We'll be there."

They dropped me off at the library, and I mooned around, feeling anxious and useless and a little scared. I did find a pretty wonderful book of photographs of chickens—rich, luxurious, fancy fashion photo shoots of champion show chickens (who knew?). I bet Maggie would help me set up some kind of drapery or curtain for background, and we could capture each girl individually . . . just when I thought we'd gotten away with Len's cancer, why the hell did we have to get more scared? And I hadn't even talked to Travis about Mr. Olmitz or giving Len the watch or anything.

But they looked happier when they picked me up with my chicken book. One of those little slits looked a little angry, the doc had said, and he gave Len a slug of a different antibiotic and another prescription. If he got worse, we'd call up the docs in Kansas City, but the doctor wasn't too worried yet.

By evening, Len felt better. Maggie dug up an old red velvet bedspread and a green tapestry sort of curtain, so we were hatching plans to stage our hen photo shoot. Len thought we were crazy, but chuckled in a tolerant sort of way.

"Can we plug in a lamp in the barn for some more light?" I asked.

"I'm sure I have one someplace we can use," said Maggie. Then her head snapped up and she said, "Oh hell."

"What?"

"I totally forgot till just this minute . . . Pastor Dave called and said some folks at church had brought him some stuff for us—cookies or casseroles or something—and he had it in the fridge at the church."

"So you can just pick it up tomorrow, right?"

She sighed. "I just feel like . . . I'm not up for that right now. Len needs to rest, I'm exhausted, and sometimes . . . sometimes people being nice to you is harder than when they aren't. They're being wonderful and sweet and all, but . . . I wish . . ."

I picked up my cellphone.

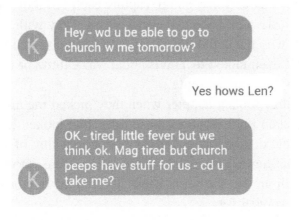

K: Hey - wd u be able to go to church w me tomorrow?

Yes hows Len?

K: OK - tired, little fever but we think ok. Mag tired but church peeps have stuff for us - cd u take me?

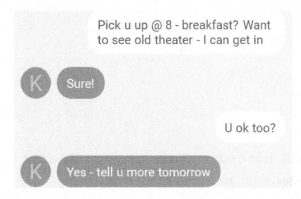

Pick u up @ 8 - breakfast? Want to see old theater - I can get in

K Sure!

U ok too?

K Yes - tell u more tomorrow

"All set," I said. "Travis'll take me. He's going to pick me up early, we'll go to Ginny's first, then go to church for the 10:30 service and pick up your stuff. How's that?"

Maggie sighed again, but she was smiling "You are a doer and a shaker, aren't you?" she said.

"Like her dad," said Len from the doorway.

I'm pretty sure he meant that in a good way. I hoped so.

The watch chain was clipped around his belt loop. The watch was in his pocket.

Chapter 24

I had biscuits and gravy. Travis had his skillet. Joan wasn't there.

"She worked late last night," he said.

"Late? Ginny's is only open till eight, I thought."

"Oh, she tends bar over at the Silver Moon a couple nights a week. She gets home at like three in the morning, and swears she isn't going to leave the house at all on a Sunday if she doesn't have to."

No wonder she looked tired.

"So, you must have to babysit Doug kind of a lot."

He nodded.

"His best friend's mom helps out sometimes too, but . . ." He trailed off and fidgeted his coffee cup till it fitted exactly inside the bank logo on the paper placemat.

"What happens when school starts again? Or, wait . . . are you graduated?"

He shook his head.

"I should be. But I lost a bunch of time out of school after the fire, so I gotta go back. They were pretty good about it. I just need a couple classes. I'll be done by Christmas."

"You couldn't do summer school?"

"Only at the juco, and . . . and it didn't make sense to spend the money on the tuition if I could finish up for free."

Juco? Juco . . . oh. Junior college.

"Not like it matters," he said, slowly turning the coffee cup around and around. "Not like I'm going anywhere anyway."

"I'm sorry," I said. "I wish . . ." I didn't know what to say. Len had talked about the scholarships gone, no way to pay, he couldn't even play sports . . . I felt so bad. I almost reached out to touch him, but somehow felt like he wouldn't like it. He looked miserable. Like Maggie said—sometimes people being nice to you made you feel even worse.

"Come on," he said. He was shaking it off. "You got your camera?" I picked up my bag and followed him out the door. It was hot, thick-aired and muggy. Off to the southwest, the sky was a deep purple wall.

"Storm down that way," said Travis.

Around to the alley, in the back door, down the stairs into the cool, dim underground. As we passed through the old bar, he laughed a little and said, "I'll buy you a drink on the way out."

He dug into his back pocket and pulled out a snub-nosed screwdriver. He twirled the screws out of the hasp on that other door in seconds.

"I undid the screws earlier," he whispered. "Watch your step, it's dark in here."

A wide, low-beamed space, and yeah, it was dark. Travis slid on the flashlight on his cellphone, and I tripped mine too. I followed him to the back, to a rusted little iron spiral staircase. We clanged up the steps, ducked through a warped door and into the theatre. In the flaring, swaying lights, we padded down the sloping side aisle on the dust-clogged carpet toward the stage. I played the beam around, along rows of crooked, broken seats, then up over plaster medallions on the walls, once brightly painted, and now faded, busted, and crumbling.

"It was pretty fancy once," said Travis.

"A miniature movie palace!" I said. "This is great!" A decrepit stage curtain still hung there, ribboned by its own weight and spiders. Good thing I don't mind spiders. A derelict couch slumped at one side of the stage, with a leaning metal floor lamp beside it. I was surprised when Travis twisted the switch and it came on, casting a yellow pool of light and waking up the shadows in the seats.

"A little secret wiring job," he said. "I've been coming here. Off and on. Just to kind of relax, have some time to myself." He dropped onto the couch, puffing dust out of the cushions.

"Len said . . ." I stopped. Maybe I shouldn't go there. But I did anyway: "Len said your dad . . . your dad was the one who set the fire? Not on purpose," I added. Travis stared over my shoulder.

"Yeah. He was . . . yeah, he was cooking meth in the bathroom. I guess a lot of people know about it."

"Was it bad? I mean, living with him, doing that?"

"Yeah. It was . . . it sucked. When Doug was little, he used to be gone for long periods of time. He'd get jobs on oil rigs or pipelines or something, and be gone for like months. We were almost normal then. But one time he came back and he'd found meth on that last job. He'd get and lose jobs like crazy, jobs here and there, finally got a job out at the meat processing place between here and Larned. The meth let him work double shifts for weeks. He couldn't buy enough, so he started making it. It was bad."

114

"How did your mom put up with it?" I asked. I felt sick for her, for him.

He snorted. "She had two kids, and if she opened her mouth, he shut it for her."

"My God," I whispered. "Oh, Travis, did he hit you too? And Doug?"

"Not so much," he answered. "We were kind of beneath his notice. Until . . ." He went quiet.

"What happened?"

Again, that faraway look . . . what I read about once called "the thousand-yard stare" that soldiers would get sometimes.

"Last year sometime. He was after my mom," he said finally. "He had her in the bedroom and I could hear her crying and begging him to stop, and he was roaring at her. Dougie was screaming, he was so scared. I picked up my baseball bat and I busted in the door. He took one look at me, and cranked as he was, he stopped. After that, he just came and went, did what he wanted, but he didn't bother us like that again. I know this is bad, but I am so glad he's dead, I can't tell you. Even if we live in a crappy house trailer, even if I work at the tool rental counter the rest of my life, even if Mom has to work all the time . . . we're okay. We'll manage." He paused. "Sorry. That's my sad story. Didn't mean to bring all that up. But I guess you should know. About me and all that crap. Like I said, not from the best stock."

"I can see why you'd come here," I said. "Quiet and all to yourself."

"I like to imagine what it was like, all painted up and fancy and full of people, waiting for a show."

"Chicago had a lot of big old movie palaces," I said. "Most of them are gone now, or else they're fancy live-show theatres. This is so . . . cozy. It's nice a little town could have this grandiose place on a small scale. And now it's all deserted and dusty . . ." My eyes wandered. I opened up the aperture on my camera and took a shot out into the lopsided rows of empty seats, then prowled out to close-up a broken pair . . . the crumbled plaster orna-ment . . . a surreptitious shot of Travis hunched on the couch in the lamplight, at the edge of the empty stage. I focused on a cracked vase with cobwebbed plastic plants still in it . . .

"Strong men tremble when they hear it!"

What the . . . ! A thundering baritone voice behind me, rough-edged and gravelly, made me jump.

Travis was standing in the middle of the stage, glower-ing, shoulders thrown back, fists clenched.

"They've got cause enough to fear it!"

Travis Gibb was up there, belting out the entrance song of Bill Sikes, the villainous Bill Sikes from the mu-sical *Oliver!* Without even thinking, I raised my camera and squeezed off two shots, and then punched the camera into video mode. Where did this come from?

He paced, he bellowed, he menaced, he stormed, his boot heels cracking across the dry wood floor. This tall, lean kid in jeans and a baseball cap . . . he just *became* this brutal, violent burglar, the murderer straight out of Dickens. And his voice . . . it boomed, it crashed, it rolled out to the back row.

He stopped. He stood there, alone on the stage, stuck his hands in his pockets, and kind of shrugged at me.

"Sometimes I do this here too," he said. I shut off the camera, scrambled up onto the stage, and stood in front of him.

"That was . . ." I struggled. "Jesus, Travis, that was beyond amazing. Does anyone know you do this? You're . . . that was incredible." Incredible. Amazing. Awesome. All those words that people use every five minutes, and then you have nothing left when you need a word like that.

"My mom," he said, laughing sheepishly. "We sing 'em together. Told you, I know a lot of them by heart by now."

With his hands still jammed deep in his pockets and that nervous half-smile on his face, he opened his mouth and softly, softly, sang: "*There were bells on the hill . . .*"

I sucked in a shaky breath and froze. Travis stood there and sang that sweet, sappy, gorgeous song to me. Silky, liquid, rich, gentle, with a smile in it, not a note wrong. To me. Then he took his hands out of his pockets, took mine in them, raised them and kissed my knuckles. And camera or not across my chest, he pulled me in and kissed me.

I didn't worry about my lips or my teeth or how to hold him or how to breathe, it was just this sweet breaking wave of joy. We kissed and we breathed and we held onto each other.

And then the siren went off.

Travis's head snapped up.

"That's the storm siren," he said. "We need to get downstairs. Now!"

He vaulted off the stage and pulled me after him, then shoved me ahead of him up the aisle, down the iron staircase. I fumbled with my cellphone and got the flashlight on, and we dove into the next room, into the windowless alcove behind the bar.

The wind was howling. I could hear it even from down there. I had to raise my voice: "Is it a tornado?"

"Maybe," he said grimly. "That sky looked ugly before." He crouched in the corner. "Get down, come on." I folded up, and he gathered me in. I pressed into his chest, and his heart was thumping. So was mine. I was too scared to cry, so I just clutched at him and shivered.

The wind thundered, the window in the main room rang and shuddered. Travis ducked his head over mine, wrapping his arms over us as best he could. People always say "roared like a freight train," but in Chicago, the freight trains are generally blocking street crossings going about five miles an hour, so they just kind of grumble. This wasn't like that. You couldn't hear anything but *it*, this huge whoosh and thunder . . . Was it a minute? Five minutes? Fifteen? I have no idea. And then it stopped. Just stopped. Some rain slapped the window, and in a minute, even that stopped and was just a gentle, normal rain patter.

I was afraid to come out of there. Not for what might happen to us, because we were okay, but what would it look like . . . upstairs?

"Shit," Travis was saying. "Come on, you piece of shit!" He was frantically punching his phone, but it was like one of those dreams I have sometimes, where no matter what you push, the call won't go through, it won't ring, the phone is dead.

"My mom, Doug . . . they're at home . . . in a damn trailer park!" We ran.

We blundered through a dozen pale people in the basement under Ginny's—people with napkins still in their collars, the cooks in their greasy aprons, our waitress crying in the arms of a middle-aged woman. Travis hit the door out into the alley, but it wouldn't open. He shoved and kicked, and one of the cooks came up after him and together they muscled it open, forcing aside the dumpster that had been jammed against it. Trash cans were rolling, debris blowing down the alley and across the parking lots. A metal sign went cartwheeling across. But the cars and trucks were still parked, and the buildings were still standing. There, anyway.

We got into the truck. People were coming out of the buildings on the street, peering and looking around. A tree in a planter had been driven through the window of the insurance agent's office. Travis peeled down the street and onto the highway, swashing through lakes halfway across the road, veering to miss tree branches scudding across the asphalt. I started to see bigger trees down, a long row of cottonwoods ripped up and toppled. He turned off the main road onto another blacktop, and as we got away from the main road, things looked better. The wind had died, the rain was just a drizzle. He pulled in the gate of the mobile home park and slowed down as people were wandering, gathering, talking, taking stock. There was a woman sitting in a lawn chair with a blanket over her shoulders, holding a beer and a tiny chihuahua in her shaking hands, as the neighbors surveyed the huge tree branch embedded in the roof of her trailer. One guy was already firing up a chainsaw.

Travis hit the brakes in front of an intact trailer.

"Oh thank God," he muttered as he leapt out. His mom met him at the door. He hugged her tight.

"We're okay," she kept saying. "We're okay. It passed us by, just the big winds. We saw it, saw it hang out of the sky, and skip on east. Is it okay in town?"

"It was like a big elephant trunk!" cried Doug. "A giant gray elephant trunk, just hanging and whipping!"

Maggie. Len. They were east of town.

Travis! Take me home!

Chapter 26

"I'm so glad they're okay," I said.

"Me too," he said.

Neither of us said another word. Travis pushed that old truck till it rattled, heading east on the highway, rocking the corner by the liquor store and up the blacktop, out of town. More trees down in the shelterbelts. They had the weather radio, they'd be down in the cellar. They'd be okay. They'd be fine. They'd lived here all their lives, this was no big deal, they'd be fine.

Travis hit the brakes. A telephone pole snapped off at the ground, tilted nearly horizontal, held up only by the wires, lay nearly across the road. He slammed into reverse, turned around, headed back to the next crossing, turned, spat gravel as he accelerated. We squared off the next mile and came back out, and backtracked.

The tall yellow house was right there, right where it should be. Maggie burst out the door as I burst in—we practically blasted right into each other, and we both laughed to keep from crying.

"I was so worried," "I was so scared," "I'm so glad you're okay," "Thank God you're all right . . ."

"Is everything okay in town? Is Travis's family okay?"

I told her what we'd seen, what we'd done, that they were all okay. Seemed like the storm had decided to leave Opulence be for now.

Travis came in with Len, who'd been checking to see if the roofs were still on the garage, the sheds, the barn, the house . . .

"Late in the season for a tornado. One big tree down on that fence beyond the barn," he said. "We got another fence to fix."

"I'm in," I said.

"Me too," said Travis.

"Well," said Maggie. "I feel like I need a drink, but ten in the morning is a bit early for me."

"You still want to go over to the church?" Travis asked me. "We can make it before the service starts."

"Aw, sweetie, you don't have to if you don't feel like it," Maggie said. "I can call Dave and tell him we'll be over tomorrow sometime."

"It's okay," I said. "We can go."

"You sure?"

"Yeah." I was kind of brimming over with thankfulness, and I mostly wanted to get back in that truck with Travis Gibb.

So we did. He backed out of the drive, went a hundred yards up the road, stopped the truck, pulled me over and kissed me again, hard.

"I have been wanting to do that so bad for a long time," he said. I stayed slid over next to him, his arm tight around my shoulders.

We came up to the corner where the church was from behind it. There was too much space in the wrong place. Something wasn't right. There were cars and trucks parked any which way, people were wandering and gawping, like at the trailer park. When we walked around in front . . . Pastor Dave was standing in his jeans and a

T-shirt, his graying hair sticky and windblown, his face redder than usual, by the bushy old cedars and tipping his head back, staring up at what wasn't a steeple any more. Bricks had rained down all over the place, piles of bricks and mortar and broken beams. A chunk of roof was gone, and two tall windows below empty and jagged.

"Thank the Lord," he was saying to the men clustered around him. "It was early and no one was inside." Then he laughed. "Well, I guess we'll be having services in the fellowship hall for a while. Or out under God's own trees and sky. Bring your own lawn chairs!"

A burly man pulled up in a cement-spattered truck and hauled out several wheelbarrows. People started randomly gathering up the wet bricks, tossing them into the wheelbarrows, stacking them off to the side. What else was there to do?

I was hanging back. I wasn't going to bother Dave now about our casseroles. But Travis strode over to him, clasped him by the hand, gripped his shoulder and said, "Let me know if I can help. I'll ask my boss about getting you some tarps." Dave wrung his good hand.

"Bless you, Travis Gibb. Is that Katie over there? Is everyone okay by you?"

"Yes, we're all good. No real damage in town that we saw, either. I'm really sorry, Reverend."

Dave shrugged and smiled, his face going even more red.

"Look at all the help I got already," he said, waving his arm at the folks picking up bricks. "You two need to pick up your food . . . Go on around to the back of the extension there to get into the kitchen . . . it's all solid back there." And he turned to talk to a woman whose family construction firm would give him some scaffolding when he needed it.

We opened the fridge inside and stacked up the Pyrex and the Tupperware: tuna fish casserole, macaroni and cheese, lasagna, barbecued pork, a sack of oatmeal cookies (we ate half a dozen of them), a carrot cake. There were cards attached to most of the containers. Poor Pastor Dave.

A boy stuck his head in the door.

"You Katie? The one who takes pictures? Pastor Dave wants to know if you'll take some, for the record, he said."

"Sure," I said. "I can take some now if he wants, my camera's in the truck."

Travis loaded up the food and I started shooting. The sun came out, the puddles glistened. I shot the tall arched gaping window. I shot the broken base of the steeple. A little girl clutching a brick by a wheelbarrow. The seven-foot cross from the tip of the steeple caught upside down in the trees. I got one of Pastor Dave with the sheriff, both standing with bowed heads by a cascade of fallen bricks.

Travis was talking to a woman in a sweatshirt and jeans with a notebook in her hand. When he spotted me, he waved me over.

"This is Ms. Terrence," he said. "My English teacher last semester."

"And moonlighting for the *Opulence Leader-Tribune*," she said with a grin. "Nice to meet you, Katie." I shook her hand. That was the little undersized paper I saw once or twice a week at the grocery store. At least they still had a newspaper.

"Did you get some shots?" she asked me. "Can I see?" I handed her my camera and she flicked through them on the screen.

"If you can get them downloaded today, would you send me the jpegs? Might be something we could use." She tore a sheet out of her notebook and scribbled her email address on it.

Surprised, I said, "Sure, I guess."

Travis raised his eyebrows and made a "Wow!" face at me.

"I'll get them to you right away," I said. "Thanks!"

On the way home, I finally got to tell him about the watch. And about Mr. Olmitz.

"I'm sorry," he said. "But I'm glad he got the watch done. And that it made him happy to do it."

Maggie helped us bring in the food, and fussed about how people shouldn't have, and about keeping the cards and the containers so she could give them all back again, and should this go in the freezer or should we have this today?

Travis sauntered into the living room with me.

"So," he said to Len. "I hear you got this watch."

Len squinted up at him. "You in on that?"

"Along for the ride," said Travis with a shrug and a grin and a sideways look at me.

Two days later, the photo of Pastor Dave and the sheriff was on the front page of the *Leader-Tribune*. They paid me twenty bucks.

It had been a hell of a week.

Chapter 27

TO: pammyrdal@. . .
FROM: kmyrdal@. . .
RE: video and question
07/02 9:47 pm

Hi, Mom—I just posted this video—the link's at the
bottom. It's a guy we know here, a super nice guy, and I
think it's pretty amazing. Sorry about the crummy video
quality, but it was kind of spur of the moment. I was
wondering about the arts college—do you have to audition to apply? He might be interested, but he has this
not great family situation and there's like no money. Are
there scholarships he could apply for? No hurry or anything, just thought I'd ask. Tell me what you think about
the video! Love, K

TO: kmyrdal@. . .
FROM: pammyrdal@. . .
RE: Re: video and question
07/02 10:15 pm

Hi, honey—Wow. I am impressed, crummy video or not.
He's really good! They do the application process all
online—www.chiartscoll.edu. Forms there for financial
aid too. He'll need to do a resume and a letter of recom-

mendation, and I think they have requirements for videos of performance—should all be on the website. Will need a better video ;-) Hope this helps.

I have a few more listings on houses—see the links below. Realtor getting ready to show this place soon. I've looked at a couple of these, tell me what you think. You'll probably like not being on the 19th floor anymore! Talk soon, love, Mom

<u>www.chiartscoll.edu</u>

Admissions / Financial Aid

Click HERE for admissions forms.

Application Requirements
Musical Theatre:

- Personal Essay
- Resume of all theatrical performance: show, role, venue
- Video of two dramatic monologues—maximum 3 minutes total
- Video of two song performances of contrasting types
- Video of 90 second dance, solo or production number

Oh. Well, maybe this wasn't going anywhere. If no one ever knew he even sang like this, he wasn't going to have a resumé, a music teacher, or theater director. I was sure he could move—he was an athlete, but dance? I didn't think one minute of Bill Sikes and "Till There Was You" was going to cut it. Still, I remembered how the hair on the back of my neck stood up when he bellowed from the stage . . . And I could do a better video, if we had some decent light . . . in the barn! We could open up the big door and do it there—the setting would be rough and dusty . . . perfect. I read somewhere about some movie star who auditioned for a musical by singing into his cellphone. What the heck—couldn't hurt to try it!

I looked at where the house listings were located. Brookfield let you have three chickens. Oak Park only two. I hoped the Western Springs one was a good option.

The Fourth of July was quiet. It had been so hot and dry that the county banned all fireworks. Some of the people in our building in Chicago would have fireworks parties, and we'd go over across the hall to the side that looked north toward Navy Pier to watch the display. The adults would drink, and we kids would eat and go "OoooooOOOOOH!" when the colors flared in the sky over the lake, and the boys would all howl and go "BOOOOOOM!" with the biggest explosions of noise. I didn't want to be out on the balcony, so I missed most of it, and would sneak back home before it was over.

There was a picnic at the church. More mostaccioli and a vat of barbecue pork from a place in town, and lime jello and potato chips and hot dogs and sloppy joes. Everyone brought lawn chairs and blankets and wandered in and out, sat under the trees or inside the fellowship hall. Maggie brought back all the Tupperware and casserole dishes, and there were lots of hugs and shoulder pats. Len felt good; he and Pastor Dave stood in the shade with beers in their hands, and I was amazed to see Dave give him a hug and him accept it. The fallen bricks had been picked up. There were bright blue tarps over the roof and some scaffolding and bracing around the base of the steeple.

I'd texted Travis and asked if he wanted to come, and he said his mom had the day off so they would probably all come. So when we came inside with all the containers, I was happy to spot Joan in the kitchen, ripping open packages of paper plates. I went off looking for Travis. And there he was, leaned back in a lawn chair with a guitar across his lap! A guitar? I didn't go over right away. I stood back and watched. He idly plucked and strummed, and a couple kids came over and said something to him. He sat forward and started to sing . . . too low for me to hear, but the kids grinned and chorused with him, and they all laughed. Then he spotted me. He shrugged and made a little crooked face, set down the guitar and waved.

"A man of many talents," I said lightly.

He shrugged again.

"My dad used to say the guitar is the easiest instrument in the world to play badly."

"Did he teach you?"

"Yeah, a few chords. Old country and western songs— most of 'em are only a few chords."

I sat in the grass at his feet. He shed that half-smile down on me and said softly, "Glad to see you."

"Me too."

We just sat there for a minute.

"Travis . . ."

"Hmmm?"

"I was just thinking . . . my mom just got a new job. She hasn't started it yet, but she's going to be working at this college in Chicago. It specializes in the arts—music and visual arts and theater and stuff. I just wondered . . . I asked her . . . they have a website with all their information and applications and scholarships on it. Maybe you should have a look at it? Like, maybe you'd be interested . . . just to look?"

Travis gazed up into the trees. Without looking at me, he said, "I don't know, Katie, that's probably not . . . for me . . . I don't know."

I sat up and set my hands on his knees and looked him in the face.

"Travis, do you know how good you are? You're amazing. You belted out that Bill Sikes number and blew me completely away. And you can do a gorgeous love song . . ."

He flushed, but he smiled.

"Don't be mad at me—I videoed part of Sikes and showed it to my mom . . . no, no, no one else! Just her! And she was really impressed. She knows about this stuff, and she thought you were awesome too. All the information is online. It wouldn't hurt to look . . . You even said, sometimes you thought about that audience in the theatre, all waiting and excited . . . you could be up there!"

"Katie!" he stopped me. "Katie, look at me! You think I'm going to fit in with the musical theatre crowd? In Chicago? And if you tell me I'm already perfect for *Phantom of the Opera*, I swear . . ."

I felt like he'd slapped me. Like when he thought I was too high and mighty to know who his mom was. And honest to God, I didn't even see the scars any more. Only when something reminded me, like he just did.

"What a shitty thing to say to me!" I barked. "How could you even *think* I would *think* such a thing about you!"

He plucked up his baseball cap, raked back his shaggy hair, red in the face.

"Maybe you should just get a haircut," I snapped. "That would help." And I got up and walked away.

I stayed away. I didn't look for him or Joan or Doug, and when I did, they were gone.

Maggie was gabbing with a hundred people. Then I spotted Len, out in the cemetery. He was just standing by himself. I went out there. I came up alongside him, and I put my arms around his waist and laid my head on his shoulder. He wrapped an arm around me.

"That's my dad," he said, pointing. "And my mother."

A red granite headstone. Leon Myrdal, 1917-1958. Theresia Myrdal, 1920-1974.

"My dad's parents are over there; one of my uncles and a couple aunts are here too, other uncles in Colorado and California. They didn't want to stay on the farm either."

There were quite a few Myrdals on the stones.

"I was eighteen when Dad passed—skin cancer. All those hours in the sun. Once your dad left, the heart kind of went out of Mama. She'd . . . lost a couple of babies between me and your dad, so it was hard on her. She died the next year."

"I'm sorry," I murmured. "But you were still there."

"I was."

"By yourself?"

"I was. Till I met our Maggie in the aisle of the hardware store. Buying a kitchen faucet."

"Really? That's how you met?"

He nodded. "She said she'd make me dinner if I'd help her put it in."

"Was she by herself too, then?"

"There had been a husband before, but it seems he was not kind to her, and she left him."

Oh. It had just never occurred to me that Maggie had had a life before. A marriage, a job, even . . . what had she been before? She seemed to be someone who was just exactly where she belonged, I had never thought of her any other way. Sort of like my mom. Who was starting to surprise me too, a little bit.

"Did you never want to leave here?" I asked him. He shook his head.

"Nope. My grandfather built that house, and I was born in it. I'm just rooted here. Maggie's a Kansas girl too."

Maybe Travis is too, I thought. Maybe this is where he should be. And he knows it, and I don't because I'm from somewhere else. But I sure didn't feel like a Chicago girl, like that was where I should stay forever and ever. Maybe my dad had given me a little country blood, without knowing it or even wanting to. And that voice, that art, that power Travis had, hidden away from everyone . . . I felt so sad. I thought we were friends. And more. And I still felt this thrill when I thought of how it felt when he kissed me and I kissed him, and when he smiled at me and said he was glad to see me.

"Travis and I had a fight," I said. "I don't know if we're friends anymore." Len's arm tightened around me.

"Don't you let that boy hurt you," he said. He sounded almost fierce.

"He didn't exactly hurt me . . . well, he did by thinking something bad of me that wasn't true. I think I hurt him somehow too, without even meaning to or knowing how not to," I said.

"Boys. Men." he said. "They walk around always hugging their pride, thinking someone's ready to burst it. Especially when they're not sure how true that pride is."

"Maybe," I said. "But I wonder . . . maybe he's sore all over, from all that's happened to him, so he's always kind of braced for more, and pushes away before it can happen."

Len looked down at me, and raised his eyebrows. "Could be," he said. "You're a smart girl, you know?"

My phone deedled a text message coming in.

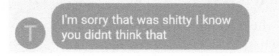

I probably shouldn't have, but I held it up for Len to see. He snugged his arm around me again.

"Good," he said. "I know he's not a bad kid. Had some tough times."

"He said to me once, sort of joking, that he was from bad stock."

Len grunted. "Hopefully his mother's side has outweighed the other."

I texted back:

Chapter 28

He did look.

"My mom says I should go for it," he said when he called.

"Yes!" I said. "But we need a better video for the songs. I wish we could get some music . . ."

"We could . . . oh, I don't know, Katie . . . maybe I could do . . ."

"What! What? Maggie and I have some lights set up in the barn where we were doing the chicken shoot."

"The what?"

"Oh, never mind, just a silly project we were doing. I thought with the barn door open with those lights, we'd have a sort of dark, rustic abstract background, which would be cool for Bill Sikes, and . . ."

"Um, well, we need two, right?"

"Yeah. Something else different."

"I have an idea . . . it'd be different, but maybe it's stupid . . ."

"No, what? Tell me!"

"I'll tell you when I get there."

He showed up with the guitar.

And no baseball cap. And hair cut short all over his head, just long enough to lay down flat. I couldn't help it, I stroked his head and grinned.

"It looks great!" It felt nice too, soft and feathery.

We futzed around in the barn, scaring the sparrows, and he asked Maggie if she had just a plain old wood chair. She loved his hair too. I set up my camera, got him in the chair with the light from the big door falling just so. He sat with a boot heel hooked over a chair rung and strummed a few chords. Then he nodded and I rolled.

He said I'll love you till I die . . .

Maggie leaned in the doorway and shook her head. In that rich voice brimming with an almost-sob, he sang this song that broke your heart while it made you smile at the schmaltz of it, about a man who only stopped loving her the day they placed a wreath upon his door.

"That," said Maggie, "was incredible. George Jones would be crying in his beer."

"You know that song?" I asked her.

"Good God, of course! One of the greatest country songs ever!"

"You think that'd be okay?" Travis asked her earnestly.

"For what?"

So we had to explain. She just glowed at him.

"You have to do this!" she cried. "You have to!" Travis smiled sheepishly.

"See?" I said to him. "See how people react to you? Now, if you can just do a dance number . . ."

Travis slumped. "Katie, there just isn't anything I can do. I can't." Maggie frowned, hands on her hips, thinking furiously.

"You have to dance?"

We nodded.

"But you're an athlete," she said slowly. "Basketball! You ran, you jumped, you spun in the air, you executed complicated plays with the other guys . . . Otis Robbins was your coach, right?"

"Yeah," he answered.

"He must have films, video, of games . . . do a high-light film! It's what, a couple minutes of layups and jump shots, some footwork . . . he'd help you, wouldn't he?"

Travis was shaking his head in amazement.

"Guess I can ask," he said.

"Ask!" she insisted. "Or I'll call him up and tell him to."

"You know him?"

"Yep," she said. "Before you were in high school, Mr. Gibb, I was the secretary to the principal. I got to know a few people." She winked.

"Maggie," I said. "You are amazing."

"I know," she laughed. And sashayed away, humming to herself.

Travis swept me up in a hug, which turned into a kiss. A really long kiss.

"You are also amazing," he said.

"I . . . I could fall in love with a guy who sang songs like that," I whispered.

He tipped his head back, let go of me and sighed. "My mom said once that she fell in love with my dad because of how he sang . . . and we know how that turned out."

"Oh, Travis, that was him. You aren't him. But maybe you got sort of a gift from him?" He made a wry face.

"You should hear my mom sing 'As long as he needs me.' She's not half bad either." He dropped back into the chair. "He was into my being a jock. He came to games, made a fool of himself, hollering and yelling at the refs. It was about the only time he paid much attention to me.

Probably just as well. After that . . . that incident with the baseball bat, he acted like I didn't exist, and I stayed out of his way as much as I could, but . . . God *damn,* I'm glad he's gone. They're safe from him now."

"So are you," I said. I put my arms around him again, and just stood beside him, and we held each other. Then the mower racketed up, and Len came cruising past the open door on the little John Deere. I jumped back, and then we kind of laughed and the moment was gone. Travis had to go to work. Celeste and Dinah came chuckling and scratching into the barn. They were maybe thinking there'd be more corn and mealworms like there had been when we were trying to make them sit up on the table for their pictures.

"We'll do Sikes another day," I said.

"Okay." He bent down and kissed me lightly, picked up his guitar and strode away in that lanky, graceful way he had.

I'm a goner, I thought.

Chapter 29

I was looking for my phone charging cord when I found the photograph. I usually threw it in the top desk drawer, but it wasn't there. I rooted around, thinking maybe I just put it in a different drawer without thinking. The big bottom drawer stuck; I dragged it all the way out, and something made a little flipping catching noise. I reached back into the recess and felt the card, caught in the back under the drawer above, and carefully wiggled it out.

A thick, square photo with colors so faded and distorted you could hardly tell what they had been once. It looked like one of those old Polaroids, from those instant cameras that spat out printed pictures in a minute or two. There were three, no, four people in the picture, squinting into the sun on a bright day. On the left was a tall young guy in a work shirt and jeans, arms loose at his side but his hands in fists, staring seriously at the camera—even scowling, looking a little annoyed, his mouth set in a short line. Next to him stood a pretty girl, also tall and slim, a teenager, maybe? She was in cutoff jeans, long legged and barefoot, her wispy bangs in her eyes, and her sleeveless work shirt knotted up at her waist. She was looking to her left, with a flirty sort of smile. Maybe she was the guy's girlfriend? In front of her was a pudgy, rumpled boy in sneakers, her hand resting on his shoulder as he looked back up at her, looking a little puzzled or curious. The fourth person, another young guy, was way over to the right, partly cut off at the edge of the picture. You could just see part of his profile, his shoulder, and part of the guitar he was carrying by the neck in his right hand. He was looking back toward the girl, with a grin on his face. It was him she was smiling at. If she was the other guy's girlfriend, no wonder he looked pissed. Who took the picture? Some kind of family picnic or something? Then I noticed in the background . . . the barn. Just one corner of it, but I recognized it—Len and Maggie's barn. So the picture was taken here. I looked again at the faces. Could the angry guy be Len? So the boy . . . was that my dad? But who was the girl? And the other guy. . . something looked so familiar . . . oh my God. Travis. The guy at the edge looked a lot like Travis. But if that was my dad, this was . . . what, forty years ago . . . even more?

I took the photo downstairs. Maggie and Len were watching the news.

"Look at this," I said, holding it out. "I found it stuck in the desk drawer upstairs. Who are these people? Len, is that you?"

Len took it from me. Maggie got up and leaned over Len's shoulder to look at it too.

"That is you, Len!" she said, smiling down at the little image in his hand. "Look how young and handsome you were . . . but you don't look very happy!"

Len gazed at the picture. He turned his head and stared out the window, tapping the edge of the photo on the arm of his chair. He didn't say anything for a minute. Maggie and I exchanged puzzled looks.

"Is something wrong?" I asked.

He sighed, deep and hard. "That's me," he said. "And the boy there, that's your dad."

"I thought it might be!" I said. "I never saw a picture of him as a little kid!"

"He woulda been about ten," Len said. "I was twenty-five."

"And the picture was here, wasn't it?" I said. "See, I saw the barn there."

Len nodded "Yeah. Mama took the picture."

"So was the girl your girlfriend?" I asked.

He looked at the photo again, gently touching the girl's face with his fingertip, and swallowed. "No," he said. "She was our sister."

Maggie and I stared at him.

"You had a sister?" we both said.

"I had an aunt?" I cried. "My dad never ever said anything about a sister."

"No," Len said. "He probably wouldn't."

"I didn't know about her either," Maggie said softly.

"And . . ." Now I was feeling nervous, upset. "And who's the guy at the edge there?"

"That was Rollie Gibb."

"Travis's father?"

He nodded.

"He was a friend of yours?" I asked, amazed.

And Len said, "No. He was not. But I couldn't do anything about it."

Maggie gently took the photo from his hand, unresisted. She ran her fingers over the faces too, over Len's grim look and the girl's pretty one.

"What was her name, Len?" she murmured.

"Cornelia," he answered in a thick voice. "After our grandmother. Cornelia Katherine. But we always called her Kate."

I had to sit down. His poor Kate. His sweet Kate.

"What happened to her?" I asked. Though I didn't think the answer would be a good one.

Chapter 30

"She was eight years younger than me," Len said. "Our dad died when she was ten and your dad was three. I was eighteen, so I had to step up. It was hard, but we did all right. For a while. When she hit her teens, though . . . the only girl, no dad, just an older brother, and she didn't listen much to me. She turned sixteen, got herself a car, one of those little VW bugs, a red one. She put flower stickers on it. It was nineteen sixty-five, you know."

I nodded.

"And then," and he took a breath, "she got mixed up with Rollie Gibb. He was twenty-two, she was seventeen. She just lost her head for him. He used to sing in one or two of the bars in town, and he'd sneak her in even though she was under age. She mooned over him. And he . . . oh, he made like she was all he ever wanted, all the while romancing every other girl in town. I tried to tell her. She didn't care. Or didn't believe me. She'd lie, say she was going to her girlfriend's, drive off in that little car and be gone till all hours. Or overnight. Mama couldn't cope. Your dad, he was just confused. He adored her. We couldn't explain it to him, he was too young." He wiped his forehead with the back of his hand.

"Then he dumped her. Told her he'd gotten a job up in South Dakota, and just left. He didn't leave a phone number or an address. He was just gone. She locked herself in her room for days. She cried all the time, wouldn't open the door, wouldn't talk to us. And then one morning we found a note on the table, to say she had to get away, she was going to Wichita, and she'd be back in a couple of days. Two days, three days, four days, no word. Mama was frantic. And then the sheriff called from Wichita. She'd showed up at the emergency room, sick, bleeding, infected. We drove down there that minute. But she died.

"She was pregnant. She found some doctor in Wichita for an abortion, and she died. Seventeen years old, pregnant, and dead. She's buried in the cemetery here. And that's what happened to her."

We sat there with nothing to say.

Maggie took his hand in both of hers. "I am so sorry, my dearest man. I never knew. I never had any idea."

"You weren't from around here," he said. "No need for you to know."

"But he came back," I said shakily. "He came back to Opulence."

"Eventually," said Len. "He was gone some years. Then his mother died, left him her little gimcrack house, and he came back and moved in."

"Did he ever . . . ever know?"

"He found out she had died. I sure as hell didn't tell him anything. But there was one day I made sure to run into him, and I told him if him and I were ever alone together some day, he better be ready because I would beat him to death. He steered clear. And . . . time went by. As it does. He got older, hooked Joan, they had their boys, he kept going out on the road for jobs . . . finally came back, and, well, you know."

I didn't dare ask: Does Travis know?

And I just kept thinking of Len seeing me with Travis, another Kate, another Gibb boy . . . it must have just been killing him. And he never said anything. Almost.

"That room upstairs, where you are," Len said, looking at me, "That was her room. I used . . . I used to bring her coffee up there in the mornings before she woke up. She didn't like getting up early."

Chapter 31

My mom always said I was a world champion sleeper, but I laid awake a long time that night, staring up at the purple-gray night ceiling. The moon shone through the trees, painting marbled patterns on the opposite wall.

God, what an awful story. 1965 . . . barely older than me, boyfriend dumps her, she finds out she's pregnant, no way to reach him, in the middle of nowhere, Kansas. I guess I'd heard stories like this, about "backstreet abortions," but it seemed like history, not really real. Even my mom had said once to me: "You have no idea what it used to be like," and she's not even that old. They had the pill in the sixties, I know that much, but I guess if you were seventeen maybe there was no place around here she could get it. And she didn't dare tell anyone? Len would have gone ballistic, her own mother . . . I didn't know. Len said their mom had "lost a couple of babies." Miscarriages? And now, I knew, he must have meant Kate as one of them. God.

And Travis. Did he know? Did I have to tell him? Did it make a difference . . . to me? Should it? It was all way before Travis was even born. Would I know if my dad had gotten a girl in trouble way before he knew my mom? I sure as hell didn't know what he'd been up to in his job . . . before . . . before he did what he did. If Travis didn't know and I told him, what would he do? How would he feel?

I felt awful. Sick, full of dread, exhausted but wound up. And Len . . . carrying that all those years. Not even telling Maggie! And *my* dad—his big sister, dead. Did my mom know about her? Even that she existed? Maybe he never told her either. Like all the other stuff she didn't know about.

And Travis. Again. Did he know? Should I tell him? What would happen if I did? It seemed to matter a lot, but to me? Him? Len. Yes.

I must have fallen asleep, finally. Only when I popped awake did I realize I had. I woke up when it was starting to get light, and someone came into my room. A tall shadow in a bathrobe, carrying a plastic insulated coffee cup.

"Hi," I said.

"Hi," said Len. "Didn't mean to wake you. You're usually out like a light this time of morning."

I sat up. "So it's been you all this time? With the coffee?" He set the cup down on the bedside table.

"Yeah." He smiled a little bit. "Who'd you think, the coffee fairy?"

"I guess I didn't think . . . maybe I just thought it was Maggie. It's been so nice, though. Thank you." He nodded. I took a sip.

"I am so sorry," I said, looking up at him. "About Kate. It's so sad. And hard. And mostly . . . mostly that you never told anyone." He sat down on the edge of the bed heavily. It creaked and squawked. "I need to ask you . . . did my dad know?"

"Yes. Your dad knew what happened. We didn't tell him the whole story till he was older. At first we just told him she got a bad infection and died from it. That's what we told most people. And if they thought anything else, well, they let us be with it."

"Daddy never said anything. I didn't know he even had a sister. I don't know if my mom knows. It's so weird, this secret."

"I think your dad just left everything here behind him when he left. Everything."

"And a lot of other stuff since," I said bitterly.

Len patted my knee with his big hand. "That's a shame," he said. "Such a waste."

I swallowed the hot coffee.

"Len."

"What, honey?"

"One more thing I have to ask. Does Travis know?"

He sat very quiet. He rubbed at his fringe of hair. He rubbed at his eyes.

"I don't know, Kate," he said finally. "I truly do not know."

"But he's a good guy, isn't he?" I said. I really needed to know what Len would say. "He's not like his dad. He's smart and talented . . ."

"So was his dad," he interrupted me. "Smart, smooth, talented, charming. And a selfish, cold-hearted sonofabitch."

"Travis isn't! He works so hard, helps take care of his brother, he helped us with the fence, he . . . he bought you that food from the Cattleman Hotel all on his own, just paid for it and packed it up so we'd have something to bring you!"

"You're right about all those things," said Len. "But you can see where I sit, right? He looks like his dad, and he's sniffing around my Kate, another Kate . . ."

"He's not sniffing around!" I cried. "He's my friend! I like him . . . I like him so much, and he likes me, and he's gentle and . . . and good with me. He's good. He made his dad stop beating up his mom, and he told me he was glad that sonofobitch was dead. That's what he said. And I don't know if he knows anything, or if I should tell him, or what to do!"

Len took the mug from my clenched hand, drew me close. I leaned my cheek into the shoulder of his bathrobe.

"I wish my dad wasn't dead," I finally choked. "He was bad, he was crooked, he lied and hurt people and stole, and made up this glamorous life we all had to live and . . . and I still wish he wasn't dead."

Len just stroked my hair with his arm around my shoulder.

I straightened up. "Or," I said slowly, catching my breath. "I just wish he was some other kind of person. And, more than anything, I wish Kate had just asked you . . . asked you to help her. And you would have. And she wouldn't have died like that."

"But we didn't get any of those choices, did we?" he answered gently. "You got us, though. And your mom." He paused. "And Travis Gibb, too. I think. I do think. It's hard as hell for me, but I do think so. I guess you got to trust yourself. And him."

He handed me back the coffee mug. I drank some.

"You didn't tell anyone, all this time," I said. "So are you okay if I tell him?"

"I don't know what Travis might already know," he said. "But if you need to, go ahead."

We just sat there for a minute. He got up.

"You go on back to sleep a while, now," he said. "It's early even for you."

"Will you make pancakes for me?" I asked. "Now?"

"I will do that," he answered. "Apricot or strawberry?"

"Apricot," I said. And followed him down the stairs, clutching my cooling coffee.

Chapter 32

I was upstairs getting dressed after breakfast when my phone bleeped. Travis.

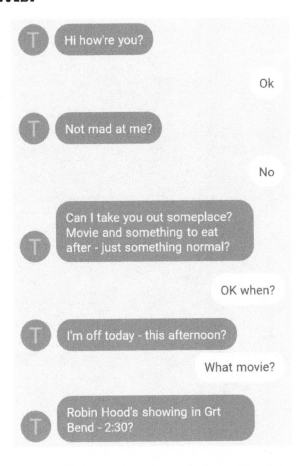

Hi how're you?

Ok

Not mad at me?

No

Can I take you out someplace?
Movie and something to eat
after - just something normal?

OK when?

I'm off today - this afternoon?

What movie?

Robin Hood's showing in Grt
Bend - 2:30?

I was going to have to deal with this, wasn't I? Like right away. Oh lord.

And then the phone buzzed.

TO: kmyrdal@...
FROM: pammyrdal@...

Hi, kiddo—I think we may have an offer on the condo soon! I guess some people still have big money to spend, and someone is interested. I narrowed down those houses I sent you but I don't want to do anything until you've seen them. So I guess we need to think about getting you home Especially if we need to get moved before school starts. You must be dying for a decent latte by now! I'll call you later and we'll talk about it, ok? Love, Mom

Nothing about today was going to be normal and ordinary.

I didn't want a latte.

When I came downstairs, Maggie took one look at me and said, "Are you okay?"

I shrugged, shook my head, bit my lip, and said, "Travis is coming at 1:30. He wants to do something normal, like go to the movies."

Maggie's shoulders fell. "Aw, sweetie, are you up for that?"

"I have to," I said. "I have to talk to him. And . . ." I took a deep breath. "Then my mom emailed. She wants me to come home."

"Already?" cried Maggie. "It's not even quite August!"

"But we may have to move, and school starts soon, and . . ."

She sighed. "I suppose that's right," she said sadly. "But . . . but we've got so we like you a little bit." She was smiling but her eyes were all shiny.

Len reached over and squeezed her hand. "That is correct. We do. But, well, we're not going anywhere."

And that's all they said.

Travis was dressed up. Well, fresh blue jeans and his boots were polished and an ironed shirt. I was in jeans, sneakers and my dad's polo shirt.

He leaned over to kiss me in the truck, and I let him. He looked sideways at me.

"You sure . . .?"

"Let's go," I said. He cocked his head and backed out of the driveway.

I didn't say anything, and he kept glancing over at me. He looked puzzled and hurt.

"Travis," I said. "Can we skip the movie? Can we go someplace to just . . . I need to talk to you about some stuff, some stuff that's come up . . ."

"Sure, yeah, okay." He drummed his thumbs on the steering wheel. "We could go down to the wildlife refuge. Take a walk or something."

"That's fine." And we neither one of us said anything more. We rolled down a blacktop, south out of Opulence. The fields were full of giant spiraled round bales of hay. Meadowlarks posed on the fence posts. Cows wandered around in pastures. We pulled off onto a gravel road through a thick green tunnel of trees that arched overhead. The cicadas were whining and singing. It was cool in the shade and hot in the sun. He parked in the trees, in the shade, and we sat there with the hot engine tinking. I got out and leaned against the truck, listening to the birds and the insects. He came around and stood in front of me.

"So, what's up," he said.

Now or never. I reached back into the truck for my bag and got out the photograph and handed it to him.

"You know who these people are?"

He peered at it.

"That's gotta be Len," he said. "I don't know who the girl and the kid are, but that . . . Jesus, that's my dad. I always thought . . . I had the idea that they weren't exactly buddies."

"They weren't. Did you ever hear that Len had a younger sister?"

He frowned, then shook his head. "I don't think so . . . no."

"That was her. She was seventeen. She fell in love with your dad." Bitterly, I added: "She liked how he sang too." He winced and looked away. "And he dumped her and moved away."

"Oh, shit," he mumbled.

"The thing is, Travis, she was pregnant. And he just disappeared. She was desperate, she went to Wichita, found some doctor . . . and she died from the abortion, Travis. She *died* because of him!" My blood was pounding in my ears, and all I wanted to do was hug him and tell him I was sorry and sorry and sorry and I love you and it's not your fault but I had to know, had to say it . . .

"Oh fuck," he said.

"And it broke Len's heart and her name was Kate."

I stood there with my hands jammed down in my pockets, shaking with cold.

He stepped up, wrapped his arms around me as I stood rigid as a tree and said into my hair, "I didn't know this, Kate, I didn't know any of it. He was wild, he bragged about all the girls he'd had, but this . . . I didn't know. I didn't know. I am so sorry. Please, Katie, don't . . . don't walk away from me. Poor Len. Seeing me and you . . . oh shit."

He let go of me, turned his back. He stared up into the trees. The leaves rattled in a hot wind with a sound like rain. Without turning around he said, "So are you saying that you and I shouldn't see each other anymore? Because of this?"

"It's not you . . ."

He groaned. "I really hope you're not going to give me the 'It's not you, it's me' speech."

"Dammit, Travis! Stop it! Stop putting things in my head that aren't there! Of *course* it isn't you, and it isn't me either! It just *is*. This horrible thing happened. I can't help that I know about it now, but how could I know and *not* know if *you* know! It affects us, affects people we care about, and I can't just go along keeping a secret like this from you. It's out in the open now. And now we have to decide what we're going to do with it. How to deal with it."

We stood there, me staring at the back of his neck, where the short feathers of shorn hair brushed the shiny stiff scars. He turned around.

"What does Len say? What did he say to you about me?"

"He said I had to trust you."

"Len said that?"

I nodded.

"Do you? Can you? Because here I am. This is me. What you see is what you get. A banged up, half-crippled clerk working at the farm supply store in small-town Kansas. Zero prospects, zero future, who'll be lucky if he gets a GED."

"But the college! Aren't you going to apply? Wasn't your coach going to help you?"

"Katie, seriously. How is that going to work? Who's going to pay the tuition? And . . . leaving my mom, going to Chicago . . . that's just not my world. I'm not even sure I want to. Why bother? Other people will have these slick videos, and years of experience in the drama club, and whatever. It's just not going to happen."

A long silence. We both stared into the dirt. The bugs whined.

"Then I guess none of the rest of it matters," I said.

He shrugged. "Maybe not."

"Especially since my mom emailed me this morning," I said, struggling with the ache in my throat and the liquid heat in my eyes. "And she wants me to come home."

And he grabbed me up, crushed me against him, and we hung onto each other for dear life.

"I don't want you to go," he mumbled. "I don't want you to leave me."

"I love you," I whispered, hoping he wouldn't hear me.

But he did. We looked at each other with wet, red eyes.

What choice did we have?

Chapter 33

I was tired of crying, tired of tears. They didn't help. They just left me with the same dry ache that never went away. So I stopped. I sat wedged into the corner of the truck seat while Travis drove me home. We neither of us said anything. It was horrible.

In the driveway, he reached for me with his scarred right hand. I took it in both mine and I kissed the knuckles, all five knuckles, three with fingers and two without. I leaned over and kissed the rough red skin on the side of his neck and he made a miserable little noise in his throat. I kissed him once, hard, on the mouth.

"I'm sorry," I said. "There's just no point." I got out of the truck, slammed the door, and forced myself to walk to the house. Maggie and Len were out in the garden, doing something with the rabbit fence. They looked our way, looked at each other, and bent back over their fence again.

Travis drove away.

The house smelled of rising bread. I went upstairs. I came back down. I dragged a chair out under the trees behind the house, near the chicken coop. Celeste and Dinah came hurrying over, figuring I would feed them. I sat down, and they twisted their little heads and focused their beady eyes on me. Celeste fluttered up onto my knee, clutching with her sharp toes, and decided to just sit there. I sat, petting a little red chicken in my lap, for a long time. Myrtle and Minnie came poking around; then Verna showed up. Bathsheba came stalking through the grass, and then Fanny and Sophie and Phoebe. Finally, just as I was wondering if I should call or go look for them, Carmen and Jane toddled into view. I still needed to photograph Sophie and Jane—they were skittish and didn't like to be held. I'd have to spend some time just following them around and get some candid shots. I gently set Celeste on the ground and scooped out some scratch for them. Snacks! They chortled and chuckled and poked and snarfed. It made me smile. Chickens will always make me smile.

In the kitchen, Maggie asked if I would trim and halve the Brussels sprouts. She had a glass of wine poured on the counter.

"Want some?" she asked me. "You look like you could use it." She poured me half a glass. It was a pale yellow and tasted like tamed grapefruit. I hated grapefruit, but I liked this.

Len came in.

"I told him," I said to the room. "He didn't know. He feels awful."

"Are you okay?" Maggie asked. I stared into the yellow wine and shrugged.

"I have to go back to Chicago," I said. "I don't know if I want to, but I have to. So . . ."

We ate chicken (store-bought, not anyone we knew personally) with Brussels sprouts and sesame seeds for supper. I went to bed while it was still light out, a little sleepy from the wine, and did not wait for sunset. I turned my phone off. I'd call my mom the next day. I'd had all I could stand for a day.

Chapter 34

"So I thought next week, Saturday? There's a flight out of Wichita at 12:30, gets into O'Hare about three. Or would Kansas City be any better?" Mom was organizing.

"Wichita is closer."

"Okay. We'll do Wichita. On Sunday, we can go look at those houses, they're not far from each other, if you want."

"Which ones are they again?"

"Western Springs, Oak Park, and there's one in Brookfield, near the zoo."

Four chickens in Western Springs, two in Oak Park, and Brookfield . . . Brookfield? Three, I think it was.

"Okay. I liked the pictures of the one in Western Springs."

"It is pretty nice . . . so, anything from your friend? About applying to the college?"

"Umm, I don't know. I don't think so. They really don't have money, and he's worried about the tuition. He also doesn't really have the experience, you know? Like he's just done this at home, with his family, not in theater class or anything. And . . . and I think maybe he's just not up for the city . . ."

"Too bad," she said thoughtfully. "He really seems talented. There are scholarships . . . well, if he's not interested . . . just thought I'd ask."

I didn't say anything.

"You there?"

"Yeah."

"It's going to be okay, Katie. We'll manage. I'll be glad to see you, glad to have you back now . . . well, now that some of the mess is cleared up. We can go get Thai food at Sawasdee when you get in. Bet you haven't had that out there!"

"No."

"Do they even have Starbucks there?"

"No. Mom, do we have a percolator?"

"For coffee?"

"Yeah. I got to like it that way."

"Umm, no, I don't . . ."

"Never mind. Maybe we can get one or order one or something."

"Sure, I'm sure we can find one online. Okay, well, listen, let me talk to Maggie, okay? About arrangements and stuff."

"Okay. Hang on . . . bye."

I carried the phone downstairs.

"My mom wants to talk to you. About me leaving." Maggie made a sad face and took the phone. I went back upstairs. I didn't really want to hear their conversation.

I opened up my laptop and starting scrolling through my pictures.

Sunset sunset sunset. Church picnic . . . Travis. The first time I'd laid eyes on him. It was still a good shot. I dug out my thumb drive and copied it over. Sunset sunset sunset. Maggie's hands in the bread dough. Church steeple. Chicken chicken chicken chicken chicken. Sunset sunset sunset. What was I going to do with all this, anyway? It just made me sad. The sunsets were drab, boring. The chickens were cute, but not much else. Not glamorous or rich or arty. Whatever. But that one of Travis . . . maybe Joan would like it. I could take it into town, get a print made . . . sure, why not. She'd like it. And he'd see it. He'd never seen it. Maybe he'd remember me from it.

Maggie was on the phone with my mom for quite a while.

She came up behind me and put her arms around me.

"We'll miss you," she said. "You'll come back, won't you? I told your mom, maybe you could both come out for Thanksgiving or even Christmas? If you wanted to?"

"Could we? I'd like my mom to see it, see the house and the chickens, and . . ."

"Yep. Definitely. Oh, look at those! You should frame some of them! Or make calendars or something! I love that one of Verna, she looks so glamorous, all spotlighted like that."

"Really? You think so?"

"Absolutely. And look how solemn and important Celeste thinks she is!"

We laughed. I guess you can't always see your own stuff very clearly. Maggie had bought a bunch of copies of the Opulence paper with my photo of the church steeple and had already put it in a frame.

"I'm really sorry about Travis," she said. "The whole thing is so damn sad. I wish . . . I wish he would just do something with himself, with his talent. I know Joan would want him to."

"His heart just isn't in it, I guess. Out of his comfort zone," I said. "I really liked him. A lot."

"And he cared for you, I could see that. It won't help, will it, if I give you the old-woman speech about you're young, you'll be okay, and all that."

I leaned my head back under her chin. "Not really. But it's good for you to say it anyway. I'll end up believing you at some point. In time."

"Yeah. Time will do that. You just have to get through it and out the other side."

"Yeah." I sighed. I missed him. I missed looking forward to seeing him. I missed how he moved, his good heart, his scars, even his prickliness. But I was going to have to leave, and he wasn't.

Chapter 35

**"Would you get some birdseed too?"
said Maggie. "The stuff in the blue bag
with a cardinal on it."**

Omelets with tomato for breakfast. It was Thursday. I
was leaving on Saturday. I was mostly packed. I wanted
to take everything with me: the eggs, the morning light in
my bedroom, a chicken (probably Celeste), the way my
pillowcase smelled after it had hung out on the clothesline, the sound of the leaves, and the smell of cows when
the wind blew from the Kirchners' place. The insulated
insurance company coffee mug was in my suitcase already. I'd created a calendar of the chicken portraits
online, and ordered several copies. I'd gotten a nice shot
of Carmen in the peonies and one of Jane dustbathing in
the driveway.

"Okay," said Len. "Katie, you want to come along?
Just for the ride."

"Okay," I said. "Can we stop at Walmart? I want to
print out one photo and put it in a frame . . ."

"Sure. Anything else?" Len asked.

Maggie shook her head and said, "Go on, get on out of
here. I'm going to mop this floor while you aren't under-
foot."

Len was waiting by the truck when I came out. He
pulled open the passenger side door—Maggie usually

drove since his back bothered him if he was behind the wheel for long.

"Here," he said, jangling the key. "You drive."

I laughed. Like when he had teased me about the chainsaw.

"Go on, get in," he said.

"But I can't drive!"

"I was driving when I was younger than you," he said. "You'll be sixteen in a month or so. Might as well get a start on these back roads."

Good God. I slid in behind the wheel.

"Lever under the left side of the seat, scooch up. Not that far! There. Can you reach the pedals okay?"

I nodded.

"Button under the column there—tilt the wheel till it's comfortable."

I did.

"Gearshift in Park—P."

"It already is."

"Okay. Turn the key, don't push the gas, just turn the key."

Rumble rumble vroom rumble.

"Press gentle on the gas . . ."

ROARRRRR!

"I said *gently!*"

Mmmble mmble ruummmmmmmm

"There you go. No more pressure than that, okay?" He released the parking brake. "Right foot on the brake. Now put the gearshift in Drive—the D. Now let up on the brake."

The truck started to roll slowly, me gripping the wheel and staring at the end of the hood as we rolled the few yards down the drive to the road.

"Brake—press, don't stomp!"

So okay, we got thrown forward a little, but I stopped. No traffic, so I rolled out, turning the wheel soooo carefully, and got out on the road.

"Now you can press the gas a little more—good, nice and smooth . . . eyes up! Watch the road, not the hood of the truck. It knows where it's going."

I was driving! I was driving the big red truck! It was amazing! It was scary but amazing!

"Stop sign up there. Foot off the gas, let it slow down on its own, then press the brake . . . there you go. Good job. Whoa, easy on the gas! You don't have to peel out of here—on this gravel, a truck'll fishtail."

I drove another mile, and another.

"Okay, stop here, no, don't pull over, nobody's coming. Just stop. Put it in Park. I'll go from here. Good start."

I buckled back up in the passenger seat.

"Should have had you shove that seat back before I got in," Len grumbled. But I was grinning.

"Thank you," I said. "That was great. Can I drive again on the way home?"

"Uh-oh," he said. "What have I started?"

At Walmart, I got the photo printed. I found a decent little matted frame that was actually wood and not plastic. I showed it to Len in the truck.

"I wanted to leave this for Joan," I told him. "Do you think she might be at Ginny's?"

"Let's go see," he said.

She was. I waited by the register—after scanning the place to be sure Travis wasn't there.

"I took this a while ago . . . I thought you might like it."

She took it and looked at it, and then laid it flat against her chest with her arms crossed over it. She couldn't say anything for a minute.

"It's wonderful," she said. "Thank you. Oh, Kate, he's so sad, I wish . . ."

"Me too," I said, before she could say anything else. "Tell him . . . no, don't say anything. Just . . . take care."

She leaned over and gave me a one-armed hug. And I hurried back out to the truck.

We got gas for the truck and I cleaned the windows. We stopped at the dollar store and stocked up on toilet paper, ibuprofen, peanut butter, and Len's favorite ice cream, which was half the price here as it was in the grocery store. Then we headed out to the farm supply store. Len dug a list out of his jeans pocket.

"Light bulbs, chicken scratch, birdseed, and . . . and what's that? I can't read Maggie's chicken scratch . . ."

"Salt? Salt for . . . oh, salt for water softener. And a faucet?"

Len sighed dramatically. "Bathroom faucet handle's been leaking. She wants a new one."

"Maybe she's reminding you that it's your wedding anniversary in September." He looked sidelong at me. "Because you met over a faucet, remember?"

He smiled then. "Eleven years," he said. "Wish I'd met her sooner. I wouldn't be such a cranky old man now, maybe."

"I doubt that," I said.

He snorted.

I loved how the farm store smelled. Earthy and grainy, with undertones of bright metal and new rubber . . . We got the light bulbs, and Len let me pick out the faucet. I hate the single-handled kind, so I got one with two white china handles. Then a stumpy, whiskery old man with giant ears came up to Len, and they started talking.

"That your niece?" the old man asked. "That'd be your brother's girl?"

"This is Kate," said Len. "She's gonna abandon us soon, head back to the big city."

"Now, what d'you wanna do that for?" the old man asked me.

"Can't help it." I shrugged. "It's where I live. But I'll be coming back, for sure."

"Here, take the cart. You want to go get the chicken and bird feed? It's over there, those aisles on the other side," said Len. "And get a couple bottles of that root beer."

I trundled off. I found the poultry aisle and dropped a bag of cracked corn into the cart. I came out of the aisle and was practically in front of the tool rental counter. And—of course—there was Travis, talking to a woman who was bringing back a rug cleaning machine. I bolted down the next aisle with the mousetraps and mothballs. I didn't think he'd seen me. The woman left, and he wiped down the machine, neatly recoiled the cord, and wheeled it off to the back. I wheeled my own cart to the other end of the aisle and snuck around that way to the bird feeding stuff. I felt shaky, and my heart was thumping. Thank God he hadn't seen me. I just couldn't deal with it. Not now. It was all over now.

I found the blue bags of birdseed, grabbed one, and heaved it into the cart. I don't know what happened, but the damn bag tore. It ripped open, and seed started pouring out, pounds of it, spewing all over the floor.

Oh, nooo! Please, please, not now! Not here! I pawed at the bag, trying to upright it so it wouldn't spill any more, but the cart was full and it was too heavy and I started to slip in the thick layer of seed spreading on the floor.

"You need some help?"

I spun around and looked into Travis Gibb's face. Mine was hot and sweating, and I almost took off running. In two strides, he reached into the cart and yanked the bag up so the tear was on top. The flood stopped.

"Cleanup in aisle ten," he said lightly. "I'll get a broom. Please, don't go. Just wait here . . ." He came back with a broom, a bucket, and a roll of duct tape. I stood there in a swamp of embarrassment while he neatly corralled the heaps of seed. "Here, hold the pan," he said. He dumped the dustpan into the bucket. "I can take this home to my mom," he explained. "She likes to feed the sparrows too." He taped up the bag and pulled it out of the cart.

"Thanks," I mumbled. "Guess I better go . . ."

He leaned on the broom handle. "So you sicced all those women on me?" he asked .

"What? What are you talking about?"

"Seriously? My mom, Maggie, your mom, the school guidance counselor . . . nothing to do with you?"

"*My* mom? How would she . . .? No! I don't know what you mean."

"Well, I guess there's been a bunch of phone calls or emails or something because my mom marched me into the empty high school where Ms. Feist was waiting for us. They're all telling me I better fill out those application forms, and the drama teacher is going to tape some stuff, so, I guess I am. When that bunch gets together, there's not much a guy can do."

"Really?" I cried. "You will? You're going to? I'm so . . . so *glad*! Will you . . . will you tell me how it goes? I mean, just email or text or something . . ."

"Can I call you?"

"Yes, yeah, sure . . . call me. I'm really glad, Travis, good luck, truly! It's a shot, you know?"

"Yeah. I mean, the worst that can happen is they'll say yes, and I can always turn it down."

"Travis! If they said yes, we'd . . . you'd . . . there'd be a way . . ."

"Yeah, well . . ."

"There you are," said Len. He was standing at the end of the aisle with a box under his left arm. "You got everything? Where's the seed?"

Travis pointed to the taped bag. "It *was* all over the floor. Damaged goods, somebody probably slit it with a box cutter when they unwrapped the pallet. Pull around back. I'll put it in your truck—no charge."

"Okay, thanks," grunted Len.

We all stood there awkwardly.

"Hey," said Travis, "You ever get that fence fixed the storm knocked down?"

"Not yet," said Len. "My carpenter's helper here is resigning."

"You going home . . . ?"

"Day after tomorrow," I said hurriedly.

Travis turned to Len. "You need a hand, let me know," he said.

"I will do that," said Len solemnly. "I will. Come on, girl, let's get going. We got a faucet to put in this afternoon."

As he turned to walk away, Travis stepped in front of him, holding out his right hand. Len hesitated. But he looked Travis in the eye and gripped the outstretched hand in his own. They nodded at each other.

Men. There should have been a hug, and every woman in the place would have cried. But they didn't, and I didn't. But before I shoved the cart after Len, I walked up and hugged Travis Gibb.

When we got to the cash register, Len set that box on the belt. It contained a bright shining steel percolator.

"Maggie told me to get one for you too," he said.

Len drove out of town, stopped, and let me drive all the rest of the way home. He made me back into the driveway. It only took me about three tries.

I filled up all the bird feeders, and scooped some corn for the girls. As I stood there and watched them peck and flap and scuttle around, I had this little fluttery feeling in my chest, and I thought of Emily Dickinson again.

Hope is the thing with feathers . . .

We did forget the water softener salt, though.

Chapter 36

Maggie and I put the faucet in. Len just couldn't lie down on his back under the sink and fiddle with the supply lines and hooking up the drain rod. So Maggie read the instructions, and I did what she said, and Len told me what tool to use and what to do when the connector was stuck. And we did it! It looked great. I admired it every time I walked by the bathroom door for the rest of the evening. *My* faucet. How about that!

"Now we're going to need to replace that dingy old vanity top," said Maggie. Len groaned. She laughed. "Next time you come," she said to me. "You can put that in too."

That night I tucked myself into the rocking chair in Len and Maggie's room in my jammies while she read a Sherlock Holmes story. We'd given up on *Jude the Obscure*; all of us got disgusted with Jude being such a wuss and just doing everything that was so obviously stupid that we agreed to let him go. So now they were working their way through Holmes, which was much more fun.

They did not let me drive to Wichita on Saturday.

I wouldn't let them come into the airport with me. We hugged at the curb. And I shouldered up my bags and wheeled that big old suitcase in before anybody cried. I did stop inside and watch the truck pull away, and then I cried.

I checked in the suitcase, and strode down the corridor to the Starbucks. Whenever I'd traveled before, Daddy always took care of everything: limo to the airport, tipping the skycap, telling us where to go and where to sit, bringing us drinks, arguing with the desk staff about the upgrade he wanted . . . It really didn't have to be so complicated. Check in, find someplace to sit, watch the notice boards, have a coffee . . . The latte was terrible—sickly sweet and barely hot. I didn't even finish it.

My phone blipped . . . Travis.

T **Safe travels**

Thanks

T **I will miss you**

Me too. Good luck let me know what happens

T **I will. When did you take that picture? Mom loves it**

First time I laid eyes on you

T **Seriously?**

Yes

T **Hope it wont be the last Kate**

Don't think so - I hope not too

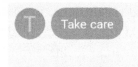

T   Take care

You too

They called my flight. I got on it, and we flew to Chicago. I had a big fat paperback of a Dickens novel Maggie gave me. She kind of hemmed and hawed, and said she wasn't sure if she should, but maybe, well . . . maybe there would be something in it I would appreciate at some point. It wasn't one I knew of, called *Little Dorrit.* But once I got on the plane, I just curled up and looked out the window instead. Flying over parts of Kansas is like flying over an abstract painting, maybe by Klee—all these colorful little patterns of the grid of roads and fields, with bright green circles where the big irrigation arms sweep around. It was kind of fascinating. It would be fun to try to draw something based on that.

It was almost startling to trudge out of the jetway tunnel into the airport. It's just so big, so noisy, so crowded, so hectic, so bright and crazy. I guess I'd forgotten.

And then I nearly walked by my own mom.

"Do I get a hug?" said this woman with a very cute, short, sleek haircut. Daddy always liked her hair long (don't guys *always* like long hair?), and she'd cut it. Her face looked thinner, she had hardly any makeup on, and she had this big smile. She reached for me and hugged me slowly, quietly, and we just kind of leaned into each other. Like we were actually really glad to see each other and were a little surprised by it.

It took forever (of course) for my suitcase to appear, and we managed to drag everything out to the parking lot, where she flicked her key fob and the lights on a steely blue Subaru Outback flashed.

"The blue Subaru! You got one!" I cried, delighted. She laughed.

"Don't tell anyone, but it's a used one . . . such a deal, when I traded in the Escalade I almost got money back," she said. "It's so cute, and so easy to drive."

"Can I drive it? Len let me drive their truck. I bet I could drive this little thing . . ."

"In time, dear heart, there'll be time for that," she said. "Look at you. All tan and healthy."

"I like your haircut," I said.

She looked almost shy. "Thanks. It feels really nice. A teeny bit of shampoo, blow it around a little and it's done. And," she added with some triumph, "I'm not going to color it any more either. So don't be horrified when the gray starts to show."

I gasped in mock horror. "No! You don't have gray hair!"

She laughed. "You'd be surprised."

We crept forward a few feet on the Kennedy Expressway.

"Are we . . . you . . . are things . . . okay?" I asked. Mom made a little face.

"Yeah," she said. "You and I, we are going to be okay." She drummed her thumbs on the steering wheel. "I heard that the woman whose job I'm filling in for— she's having twins. So if I don't screw up, I may be able to stay on. We'll see."

We rolled forward a couple of yards.

"Hey. My friend, Travis. He's going to go ahead and apply to the college. He said *you* were involved somehow. What's up with that? I don't get how that happened."

"When I was talking to Maggie, she mentioned it. And I just thought . . ." She looked at me sideways. "I guess I just thought, what would your dad do?"

I sighed. "Pull strings," I said.

She nodded. "I thought—he'd get on the phone. Find someone who knew someone . . . so I called the woman who'll be my boss. She put me in touch with someone in the admissions office, a man I'd met at a dinner one time. I sent him the link to your video. He was impressed too. He was pretty encouraging and said he'd keep an eye out for his application. And maybe some kind of audition could be arranged. And see what financial aid could be available."

"Funny how that works," I said. "In a way, I don't like it. And I don't think Travis would either, but if it gives him a shot . . ."

"It's not like we're getting special privileges for some mediocrity just because he's got connections. We're using connections to help someone who really has a talent. He really *is* good," my mom said.

"Yes," I answered. "He is."

We inched forward a car length or two.

"Mom? Can I ask you something?"

"Uh-oh," she answered, but smiling. "Will I be sorry?"

"I don't know," I said. "Sad, probably. But I already know most of what happened. I just need to know if you do too."

"Okay . . . ask."

"Did you know about Dad's sister?"

She inhaled, pressed the car forward a few more yards.

"I knew," she said carefully, "that he had an older sister, and that she died when she was not much older than you are now."

"Did he say how she died? And why?"

My mother nodded. "It was an awful story. Just plain tragic. He only talked about it that one time . . ."

"Len said he really loved her."

"Yes. He did really love her. They kept it from him a long time. He was just a boy when it happened."

"And Mom . . . my friend Travis? It was his dad—that guy was his dad. No, please, you have to understand. It's nothing to do with Travis. It was all years before his mom even met him. So . . . so you won't hold it against him, will you?"

She didn't say anything at first. The jam was starting to loosen up. There wasn't any reason for it: no accident or road work or anything, just too many cars in one place. She paced the car cautiously, gripping the wheel, frowning out the windshield.

"No," she said finally. "It's not his fault. Just like it's nothing to do with you what your father did, to himself, to us, to other people. We just have to get over the hurt and not let him . . . them . . . wreck the rest of our lives."

"When did he tell you? What was the one time?" I asked.

She sighed. "When I was pregnant with you. We were picking names. We'd agreed on Philip for a boy. But he said if it was a girl, she had to be Katherine, and we'd call her—you—Kate. And he told me why."

The traffic finally broke up and the little Subaru rolled into the city.

"It was the only time I ever saw your father cry," said my mom.

Chapter 37

Mom bought the house in Western Springs. It's a really nice old brick bungalow, with hardwood floors and oak woodwork. And the kitchen! I took a picture of it and sent it to Maggie. One wall is a wood counter with cupboards above and below, just like at Cozyburgers! I have a very cool room upstairs, with slanted ceilings and a dormer window where I put my desk. It looks out into the back yard, into the trees, a little like my room in Kansas. It's November now, so the trees are bare, but it'll be nice and green and shady in the summer. There's a corner that will be perfect for the chicken coop in the spring. Mom thinks I'm crazy, but she's willing to go along with it. I actually made a cheese soufflé for her the other day to impress her with how useful the eggs will be.

Mom's job is going well. She can walk to the train station to go downtown. The woman did have her twins, and it looks like she won't be coming back. We had to work out some stuff with the schools for me: I wrote an essay, I put together a portfolio of some of my pictures, and took two exams, and they said that was good for me to finish out the term at my old school. I can walk to my new school too, which is nice. It's way bigger, lots more students, so I could be kind of unobtrusive to start. But they have a student website, and I heard they wanted people to submit photos, so maybe I'll get involved with that.

And next week . . . Travis is coming. They asked him if he could come up for a private audition, so he's flying in. He'll do that, and we'll do a bunch of stuff in the city. I'm not sure what he'll think and how he'll feel about it, but we got some tickets to a Bears game, and Mom wangled two seats at a revival of *Jesus Christ Superstar* at the Cadillac Theatre. And I'm going to drag him through some of the Art Institute. And then . . . we're going to drive him back together, and we'll spend Thanksgiving with Len and Maggie and Joan and Dougie. Mom can meet the chickens!

One day, one week, one month at a time. No idea what will happen with Travis. Maybe they won't accept him. Maybe he'll hate Chicago. Maybe he will get in and decide to do it, and meet some glamorous, talented girl, and I'll meet some . . . some guy, somehow, or maybe we'll stay friends or . . . who knows. Lots can happen in a short or a long time. We'll just let it.

About the Author

Twenty years ago, Julie Stielstra, her husband, and their two dogs used to go camping, hiking and birding in southern Colorado. One day, while looking at the Rand McNally Road Atlas, (remember those?) she saw a blue blob north of Great Bend, Kansas, and said, "Look! A wildlife refuge! Let's see what it's like." Shortly thereafter, they stopped going to Colorado and just stayed in Kansas. Then they bought a house five miles from the blue blob that was Cheyenne Bottoms, and that's where she wants her ashes scattered, though not quite yet. The original two dogs are gone, but there are two more now and numerous cats (some Kansas natives) added to the population. And there will be chickens, pending approval of the resident barn owl.

Visit Julie at
juliestielstra.com

Read

A Meadowlark Book

meadowlark-books.com

Nothing feels better than home

While we at Meadowlark Books love to travel, we also cherish our home time. We are nourished by our open prairies, our enormous skies, community, family, and friends. We are rooted in this land, and that is why Meadowlark Books publishes regional authors.

When you open one of our fiction books, you'll read delicious stories that are set in the Heartland. Settle in with a volume of poetry, and you'll remember just how much you love this place too—the landscape, its skies, the people.

Meadowlark Books publishes memoir, poetry, short stories, and novels. Read stories that began in the Heartland, that were written here. Add to your Meadowlark Book collection today.

Specializing in Books by Authors from the Heartland Since 2014

WWW.MEADOWLARK-BOOKS.COM

Specializing in Books by Authors from the Heartland since 2014